J. G. Ballard

was born in 1930 in

businessman. After the attack on Pearl Harbor, Ballard and his family were placed in a civilian prison camp. They returned to England in 1946. After two years at Cambridge, where he read medicine, Ballard worked as a copywriter and Covent Garden porter before going to Canada with the RAF. In 1956 his first short story was published in *New Worlds* and he took a full-time job on a technical journal, moving on to become assistant editor of a scientific journal, where he stayed until 1961. His first novel, *The Drowned World*, was written in the same year. His acclaimed novel *Empire of the Sun*, first published in 1984, won the *Guardian* Fiction Prize, the James Tait Black Memorial Prize, and was shortlisted for the Booker Prize. It was later filmed by Steven Spielberg. In 1991 J. G. Ballard published the sequel to *Empire of the Sun*, *The Kindness of Women*.

From the reviews of *Low-Flying Aircraft*:

'*Low-Flying Aircraft* is science fiction in a sense that the recent novels are not, and Ballard is far more relaxed and accessible when his unnerving ideas are held within the confines of the genre. The collection includes examples of his hard-headed ingenuity (what becomes of all the child prodigies?), his poignant dreamscapes (a post-cataclysmic tour of a derelict metropolis) and his apocalyptic forebodings (intelligent, immanent energy – i.e. Godhead – is discovered to pervade all matter). This is a more equable book than Ballard has allowed himself for some time.'

Martin Amis, *Observer*

'His novels have always faithfully reflected the horrific contemporary scene of flyovers, underpasses, high-rise buildings – concrete worlds in which man is dwarfed and lost. *Low-Flying Aircraft* is a collection in which he goes much further. Ballard is a storyteller who stimulates the reader's imagination and does not remain content merely to utter terrible prophecies.'

Daily Telegraph

Works by J. G. Ballard

THE DROWNED WORLD
THE VOICES OF TIME
THE TERMINAL BEACH
THE DROUGHT
THE CRYSTAL WORLD
THE DAY OF FOREVER
THE VENUS HUNTERS
THE DISASTER AREA
THE ATROCITY EXHIBITION
VERMILION SANDS
CRASH
CONCRETE ISLAND
HIGH-RISE
LOW-FLYING AIRCRAFT
THE UNLIMITED DREAM COMPANY
HELLO AMERICA
MYTHS OF THE NEAR FUTURE
EMPIRE OF THE SUN
RUNNING WILD
THE DAY OF CREATION
WAR FEVER
THE KINDNESS OF WOMEN

J. G. BALLARD

Low-Flying Aircraft and Other Stories

Flamingo
An Imprint of HarperCollins*Publishers*

Flamingo
An Imprint of HarperCollins*Publishers*,
77–85 Fulham Palace Road,
Hammersmith, London W6 8JB

Published by Flamingo 1992
9 8 7 6 5 4 3 2 1

First published in Great Britain by Jonathan Cape Ltd 1976
Previously published by Triad Granada

'The Dead Astronaut' first appeared in *Playboy*; 'My Dream of Flying to Wake Island' and 'The Greatest TV Show on Earth' first appeared in *Ambit*; 'A Place and a Time to Die' first appeared in *New Worlds*; 'The Beach Murders' first appeared in *Rogue*; 'The Comsat Angels' first appeared in *If*; and 'Low-Flying Aircraft' first appeared in *Bananas*.

ISBN 0 586 04503 1

Set in Monotype Baskerville

Printed in Great Britain by
HarperCollinsManufacturing Glasgow

Contents

The Ultimate City	7
Low-Flying Aircraft	88
The Dead Astronaut	108
My Dream of Flying to Wake Island	122
The Life and Death of God	136
The Greatest Television Show on Earth	148
A Place and a Time to Die	155
The Comsat Angels	165
The Beach Murders	183

The Ultimate City

All winter, while he worked on the sailplane, Halloway had never been certain what drove him to build this dangerous aircraft, with its ungainly wings and humpback fuselage. Even now, as he crouched in the cockpit during the final seconds before his first flight, he was still unsure why he was perched on the steep cliffs above the Sound, waiting to be catapulted into the overlit water. The tapered wings shivered in the cold air, as if the aircraft were trying to rip open the cockpit and eject its foolhardy pilot on to the beach below.

It had taken since dawn for Halloway and his helpers – the crowd of ten-year-olds who formed an enthusiastic claque and coolie-gang – to drag the sailplane from the barn behind his grandfather's house and secure it to the catapult. By the time they reached the cliffs the other contestants in the gliding championship had been aloft for hours. From his cockpit Halloway could see a dozen of the brightly painted craft hanging above his head in the calm sky.

On the ground, by contrast, the turbulent air sweeping up the face of the cliffs seemed to have broken loose from a tornado. Exhausted by the effort of carrying the glider, the boys hung limply from the wings like a line of ballast bags. At any moment a sudden gust would sweep them all into the air together.

In front of Halloway were thirty feet of miniature railway-track and the steel cable linking the sailplane to the sand-filled trolley at the edge of the cliff which would either pull the craft apart or, with luck, catapult it into the air. Halloway signalled the boys aside, and gripped the catapult release lever in both hands. Once again he reminded himself that the Wright Brothers' first sustained flights, little more than a hundred years earlier, had also been launched by catapult.

'Thanks, everybody—now stand back!' he shouted above the wind. One of the smallest boys was still clinging absent-mindedly to the port wing-tip. 'Jamie, let go, for God's sake! *Take off!*'

As the trolley lurched forward, dragging the sailplane after it like a startled bird, Halloway felt the sudden strength of the huge wings and knew already that the aircraft would be the most successful of all those his father had designed before his death. At the edge of the cliffs the trolley hurtled down its track. Halloway released the towing cable, and the glider rose steeply, carried upwards by a cold hand, almost falling on to its back in the rush of wind. The dunes and the beach reeled away to starboard, taking the world from him. The cheers of the spectators were lost in the shrill soughing of the slipstream.

Thirty seconds later, Halloway had climbed a turbulent staircase that carried him in a right-hand spiral to a height of a thousand feet. Abruptly everything around him had become quiet. Little more than a whisper, the wind sucked softly at the fabric of the glider. The heat from the sun stung his blond skin, but Halloway ignored the pain and trimmed the glider into a stable attitude. As always, his father's design had been without error. After the first yawing subsided he began to move the glider across the sky, almost feeling his father's presence in its powerful span. The sailplane soared like a condor in the thermals, dominating the other competitors now far below. Relaxed and happy now, Halloway sat back, ready to preside generously over his domain.

Halloway had begun to build the sailplanes two years earlier. After his parents' death he had moved to his grandfather's house, and for a long while had been reluctant to return to his old home. The charred remains of the sauna where his mother and father had died lay untouched below the derelict sail of the solar energy rig. The hundreds of occluded mirrors, fused by the intense heat of the fire, towered fifty feet above the calcinated roof tiles, an all too melancholy memorial.

One evening, while discussing the annual gliding competition, which the residents of Garden City organized in order to let a little civilized rivalry into their pastoral lives, his grandmother mentioned that Halloway's father had been a keen amateur pilot during the last days of powered aviation. On an impulse Halloway borrowed the keys to the house and wandered through the gutted rooms. Only the studio and workshop, separated from the house by an arm of the canal which irrigated his parents' market garden, had escaped the fire. The shelves were filled with relics of his father's restless mind – antique gear-boxes and carburettors, mementoes of the vanished petroleum age, and the designs for a series of progressively more ambitious sailplanes. The half-completed skeleton of a small glider still lay on its trestles in the workshop.

Halloway pored over the blueprints for months, intrigued by his father's casual but clear calligraphy. The marginal jottings formed a running diary of the rich inner life of this endlessly inventive man, by a bitter irony killed beside his wife in his own home by the overloaded circuitry of an advanced solar device he had designed himself. Like some pastoral Leonardo, he had sat in his studio in the centre of this placid market garden. As the canals flowed between the greenhouses filled with flowers and vegetables, as the water-wheels turned and the hundreds of solar sails silently drained light from the sun, he had devised ever more complex tidal-energy pumps and solar batteries, refuse recycle units and windmills. His real passion, though, apart from his curious interest in old internal-combustion engines, was for these gliders.

All that first winter Halloway had examined the blueprints, feeling the contours of his father's mind in these graceful airframes and wing designs. Several of the aircraft featured extensive control-surfaces, strengthened fuselage-members far in excess of any wing-loading they might need, almost as if they were designed to carry some secret cargo. But Halloway began with the most basic of the gliders. Fortunately, the art and practice of carpentry had reached an advanced level in Garden City. Where an earlier generation of teenage boy learned to strip a carburettor or re-set a distributor, the young of Garden City were expert by the age of twelve in joining and flitching and dovetailing. Within a month his group of eager assistants had helped him to build his first modest sailplane, ready in time for the summer's gliding championship.

As he urged them on, however, watching them cut and stitch the fabric, plane and polish the struts and stringers, Halloway had known already that the competition was only an excuse. He was driven by some other need, connected not so much with his father as with the metal relics, the superchargers embedded in lucite, the fuel pumps and speedometers that lay around the studio like the ornaments of a shrine dedicated to the vanished spirit of the Otto Cycle.

Long before he became a skilled pilot, Halloway had been able to outfly his rivals, as much by pure aggression as by airmanship. None of the other competitors would rise to his baiting, let alone put up a fight. Although the championships were the climax of the year's flying, the other pilots were happy to award him the prize. When he banked and dived towards the beach, chasing the faster thermals behind the dunes, the two gliders he forced aside made way for him without complaint. Their pilots, a thirty-five-year-old architect whom Halloway was always beating at tennis, and an elderly hydrographer with a red beard, had both visited the workshop to watch the construction of this huge glider, and warned him of the impossibility of launching such a craft.

Both had been suitably impressed by Halloway's catapult. They were clearly glad to see Halloway succeed – too glad, in fact. If they had not been so naturally lacking in deceit they might have questioned his motives for building this elaborate craft – not that he would have been able to answer them – but Halloway's blond hair and guileless blue eyes turned aside any suspicion. Eager for action at all costs, yet shy and very much the dreamer, Halloway had a natural talent for rallying people around him.

At the same time, he liked to provoke the crowd. Looking down at the spectators with their picnic hampers among the dunes, the officials gazing at the sky from their canvas chairs, Halloway imagined himself as a World War II fighter ace, diving out of the sun and raking these amiable neighbours with bursts of machine-gun fire. The whole bucolic landscape of Garden City, this elegant but toy-like world of solar sails and flower-filled gardens, the serene windmills and gently nodding reduction gear of the tidal-power machines – all these cried out for a Pearl Harbour.

Surprised by this strain of aggression in himself, Halloway checked his temper. Most of the three hundred spectators he had known since childhood, intelligent, civilized and kindly people who had done their best to care for him since his parents' death, and enjoyed being shocked by his desperado stunts.

They were all watching him now, hands shielding their eyes from the sun. The coolie-gang of small boys squatted on the catapult rails, obviously waiting for Halloway to astonish them.

A mile away, across the Sound, the steep concrete walls of an artificial island rose from the sea like the hull of a cruise liner. The island was a former naval station, a collection of rusting metal buildings around a lighthouse.

Although little more than swimming distance away, Halloway had noticed that few people in Garden City were aware of the island, as if they mentally assigned it to the tower blocks of the old metropolis on the opposite shore of the Sound. The previous summer Halloway had rowed out to the island, winding through the dangerous labyrinth of tidal power pontoons and rocker arms that separated the beach from the sea. In the pump-room below the lighthouse he found the huge diesel engines that once powered the warning beacon, each the size of a steam locomotive.

But even his surprise at the enormous latent power of these metal beasts paled before his first real sight of the city. He stood on the rusting catwalk, hands gripping the rail to stop himself from diving into the cold waters of the Sound and setting off to the far shore. The vast office-blocks, many over a hundred storeys high, formed a silent congregation, more remote and yet closer to him than ever before.

Below him, as the glider climbed the thermals, the first people in the crowd were standing up among their picnic hampers, the officials waving their chequered flags at Halloway. Already they had guessed that he intended to circle the lighthouse. Halloway climbed away from them, making use of the strong updraughts that rose from the heated greenhouses, solar reflectors and rooftops, the warm canals and clay tennis-courts. Already he was looking down, not only at the naval island, but at the distant towers of the city.

When Halloway reached the naval island half an hour later the shoreline of Garden City was far behind him, the lines of solar reflectors forming strips of metallic glitter. He had meant to impress everyone by making a few circuits of the lighthouse before returning, but as he soared above the water he could feel the wind carrying him further across the Sound. At any moment it would be too late to turn back. He waited for the glider to bank to port or starboard, but the sailplane pressed on across the deep water. Already Halloway could see the canyons opening among the office-blocks of the city, an abandoned dream waiting to be re-occupied. Shadow and sunlight alternated between the buildings, as if flashing some kind of cryptic message to him. But Halloway knew that he had made his decision, and why all winter he had been building this strange aircraft.

Borne along by the fronts of warm air, Halloway and his glider made their transit of the Sound. The opposing shorelines had begun to converge, and little more than three miles of water separated the beach communities from the deserted quays and motor-routes of the city suburbs. Exhilarated in a way he had never known before, Halloway gripped the control stick with his knees, and stretched out his arms to seize the vivid air. He was not alone in the sky. On all sides flights of wild birds were crossing the Sound – pintails and white-fronted geese, mallard and harlequin duck. A colony of herring gulls moved below him, changing course when they passed Halloway as if guiding him through the crowded air. No longer hunted by the vegetarian inhabitants of Garden City, immense congregations of water birds thrived around the uninhabited shores of the Sound, in the mud-flats, lagoons and sloughs between the market settlements and the old metropolis.

Ahead of him, across the mercury surface of the sea, a collapsed suspension bridge lay like a drowned saurian in the gateway of the Sound. The last of the market gardens gave way to uncultivated scrubland. The canals petered out among the sand-hills. Ten miles from the city, by some unwritten rule, as if they were aware that the physical spell of the metropolis might still intimidate them, the last inhabitants to leave their factories, offices and apartment houses had marked out a no-man's-land to separate themselves from their pasts. Halloway remembered his grandfather's lurid account (the old man was only too keen to be tricked into these reminiscences) of how the city, like a thousand others around the globe, had gradually come to a halt and shut itself down for ever. When the world's reserves of fossil fuels had finally been exhausted, when the last coal silos were empty and the last oil-tankers had berthed, the power-stations and railway systems, production lines and steel-works had closed for the last time and the post-technological era had begun.

By then, twenty-five years earlier, there had been few people left anyway. By some unconscious perception of their own extinction, the huge urban populations of the late twentieth century had dwindled during the previous decades. Halloway's parents had been among the last to leave, abandoning their apartment – the only one still occupied – in one of the high-rise blocks that Halloway could see now emerging from the haze beyond the ruined suspension bridge. Perhaps it was this long-postponed departure that had separated his father from the other inhabitants of Garden City. The small but determined parties of colonists – doctors, chemists, agronomists and engineers – had set out into the rural backwaters determined to build the first scientifically advanced agrarian society. Within a generation they, like countless similar communities around other major cities, had successfully built their pastoral paradise, in a shot-gun marriage of Arcadia and advanced technology. Here each home was equipped with recycling and solar-energy devices, set in its own five acres of intensely cultivated market garden, a self-supporting agricultural paradise linked to its neighbours by a network of canals and conduits, the whole irrigated landscape heated and cooled, powered and propelled by a technology far more sophisticated in every respect than that of the city they had abandoned, but a technology applied to the water-wheel, the tidal pump and the bicycle.

He had reached the western limits of the Sound. A thousand feet below was the broken back of the bridge. Halloway circled a large ceramics works on the southern shore, letting the hot air reflected from the roof-tiles lift him as high as possible before he made the crossing to the city. The downtown office-blocks and apartment-houses were still nearly ten miles away, but facing him across the bridge was a built-up area of dockyards, suburban department stores, car-parks and motor-route intersections. Moored to the quays were line upon line of rusting freighters and oil-tankers, their hulls like husks.

For the first time, as he steered the glider across the bridge, Halloway could see the cars, hundreds of the dusty vehicles lining the quaysides, parked in the empty side-streets on flattened tyres. Immense roads ran everywhere, causeways of steel and concrete that moved like some kind of serpentine sculpture through complex interchanges. Traces of these broad decks, never less than six lanes wide, were still to be found in Garden City—on an intact half-mile section behind his grandfather's house the inhabitants staged their annual bicycle rally.

Needless to say, there were no cars in Garden City. If there had been, Halloway often thought with a kind of blank bitterness, his mother and father would still be alive. Despite their severe burns, they might still have been saved by the intensive-care unit at the hospital three miles away. The fastest transport available had been the village fire-appliance. This brilliantly designed land-yacht, fitted with the most efficient system of metal sails ever devised, and with an advanced magnetic suspension invented by a local electrical engineer, achieved a top speed of six miles an hour. By the time they reached the hospital, their distraught son tearing at the aluminium sails in a frenzy, the Halloways were already in deep shock and died the next day.

As he crossed the ruined bridge, losing height in the cold air over the water, Halloway counted the cars in the parking-lots along the quays. Scores had been abandoned on the bridge approach-roads when their owners set out on foot. The salt air had stripped away their roofs and body panels, exposing the engines and steering gear. Halloway had seen automobile engines before, in the encyclopaedias of industrial archaeology at the village school. Once, as a boy of ten, he had entered his father's workshop and found him running an old gasolene engine. The violent but controlled noise, the juddering motion that shook the work-bench and timber walls, and the heady fumes like a black gas – an intoxicating smell at once dirty and exhilarating – had almost knocked him off his feet. What he remembered above all, before his father switched off the engine and crated it away for the last time, was the overwhelming energy of this machine, the power and excitement beyond anything else in their sophisticated Arcadia. And yet, as his father told him, this was no more than the power unit of a small lawn-mower.

Not that there was any taboo against gasolene engines, nor for that matter against oil- or coal-fired steam engines. There was merely a tacit understanding that for two hundred years proto-industrial man had pillaged the earth's natural resources, and these relics were unwelcome reminders of an unhappy history. Beyond this were boredom and indifference – the inhabitants of Garden City were aware that their technology, their advanced horticulture and their casual winning of energy from the sun, the wind and the tides, had progressed far ahead of anything the age of oil and coal had achieved, with its protein-hungry populations, its limitless pollution of air, soil and sea.

By the time it reached the opposite shore the sailplane was barely three hundred feet above the metal-strewn water. The ragged edge of the eight-lane roadway passed below Halloway, the lines of cars forming bowers of rust from which a few sea-flowers flashed their blooms. Huge numbers of pigeons had taken over the silent city, and Halloway could almost believe that he had entered a vast bird-sanctuary. Thousands of starlings clustered among the seats of a deserted sports stadium. Generations of thrush and blackbird had nested on office window-sills and in the seats of open cars. Halloway had to bank sharply to avoid a pair of swans struggling to gain height above a row of dockyard cranes.

Barely clearing a warehouse roof, the glider rose again in the warm air lifting from the hot concrete of the roads and parking lots. A maze of telegraph wires straggled across the quay-side streets. Halloway flew on above the rusting customs sheds, and crossed the tidal basin of a silted-up dockyard, where a boom of freighters sat in a few feet of water. Beyond a silent railroad station, where ranks of trains stood in waist-high grass, he approached the outskirts of an urban centre, one of a dozen satellite cities on the perimeter of the metropolis. Everywhere there were stores filled with domestic appliances, furniture, clothing and kitchenware, a glut of merchandise that Halloway had never anticipated. In Garden City there were few stores—everything one needed, whether a new solar-powered kitchen stove or a high-speed bicycle, was ordered direct from the craftsman who designed and built it to one's exact needs. In Garden City everything was so well made that it lasted for ever.

Following the main arterial highway which led towards the next satellite city, Halloway crossed an area of tract housing and single-storey factories. In the open fields a local manufacturer had dumped what appeared to be a lifetime's output of washing machines. Line upon line of the white and chromium cabinets stood in the sunlight.

Warm air rose from this field of metal, carrying the glider high above the concrete embankments of a cloverleaf.

Directly in front of Halloway there was a flash of light in the glassy face of a 15-storey office building. Out of this sunburst huge wings moved in the bright air. A powerful aircraft, with a wing-span as large as his own sailplane's, soared straight towards him. In panic, Halloway plunged the glider into a steep turn, cursing himself for entering the air-space of the city, with its empty towers guarded by aerial demons. As the glider banked across the face of the office building his opponent also turned. His long wings, built to the same plan as Halloway's, were raised in a defensive gesture. A hundred feet apart, they soared together along the curtain-walling, the pilot's white face staring at Halloway in obvious alarm.

Without warning, this timid intruder vanished as suddenly as he had appeared. Turning back, Halloway circled the streets around the office block, searching for any sign of the rival sailplane. Then, as he passed the office block with its mirror-glass curtain-wall, he realized that he had been frightened by nothing more than his own reflection.

Delighted now, Halloway soared to and fro across the face of the building, playing the fool and happy to mimic himself, wingtip little more than ten feet from the curtain-walling. He waved at his reflection, holding the control stick with his knees, proud of his skill and glad to be able to show off to himself. He rose above the building on the strong currents lifting from the metal roofs of the cars, and then plunged towards himself in a 100-m.p.h. dive, swerving away at the last moment, wingtip punching out a section of the mirror.

'*Olé* ... !'

His shout of glee was lost in the splintering glass. On his third dive, as he plummeted downwards, he no longer cared when a gust of wind drove him laterally across the streets in a storm of cigarette packs. Out of control, the sailplane was hurled against the curtain-walling, knocking out a dozen windows. Colliding with his own image, Halloway fell with the broken machine among the cars a hundred feet below.

An hour later, Halloway left the crashed glider lying at the base of this huge rectilinear mirror and set off towards the towers of the city five miles away to the south-west.

Protected by the buckling wings, the cockpit of the glider had fallen among the vehicles parked outside the entrance to the office block. Hanging upside-down in the harness, Halloway punched out the fractured canopy, released his straps and lowered himself on to the roof of a green sedan.

Too shocked to do more than glance numbly at the face of the building which had dashed him from the air, Halloway had climbed across the splintered wings of the glider. Picking a car at random, he lay down in the rear seat. In this warm, stale air, almost unchanged for thirty years, he rested quietly, massaging his bruised chest and shoulders. The domed cabin of the car, with its softly sprung seats and antique contours, its raw metal functionalism, was a fitting womb to guard his passage from the open transits of the sky to the hard and immobile concrete now surrounding him on all sides.

Already, though, when he stepped from the car after an hour's rest, Halloway was coming to terms with the scale and character of the cityscape into which he had fallen. Display signs proliferated everywhere like some voracious metal flora, untrimmed and uncontrolled. The crudeness of the asphalt and concrete streets compared with the tiled and flower-decked pathways of Garden City, the elemental technology of power cables and ventilation shafts, had all the anarchic strength of a proto-industrial society, closer to the massive cantilever bridges and steam engines of the great Victorians than to

Halloway's image of the Twentieth Century.

A mile to the north-east a line of rusting cranes marked the shoreline of the Sound. If he walked through the side-streets he could reach the ruined suspension bridge in less than an hour, cross the channel by swimming from one section to the next, and be home by evening.

Without thinking, Halloway turned his back on the shore, on the cranes and rusting freighters. For all their apparent menace, the cluster of skyscrapers offered more security to him than the pastoral world of Garden City with its kindly farmers and engineers. Somewhere among those tall buildings – on the topmost floor, he was certain – was the apartment in which his mother and father had lived. As for any worries that his grandparents might have for his safety, Halloway was sure that they, like the crowds on the beach, knew only too well where he had gone.

Halloway climbed over the broken-backed fuselage of the glider. He stared at the wreckage, thinking of the months he had spent building the craft. Lying here at the foot of this mirror it reminded him of the body of his father stretched out below the solar reflector in the burnt-out ruins of his house.

'Come on! Forget it, Halloway!' With a whoop, Halloway leapt over the tailplane and set off along the street. Shouting to himself, he ran in and out of the cars, pounding on the roofs with his fists. He was going home.

For the next two hours, as the sun drifted across the Sound, Halloway pressed on down the long avenues that carried him, block after block, into the heart of the metropolis. The office-buildings and apartment-houses grew larger, but the centre of the city remained as distant as ever. But Halloway was in no hurry, far more interested in the sights around him. His first feelings of nervousness had gone. Curiosity devouring everything, he ran past the cars that sat on flattened tyres in the roadway, skipping from one side of the avenue to the other when something caught his eye. Many of the stores, bars and offices were unlocked. In a hairdressing salon—an Aladdin's cave of chromium gadgetry, mirrors, thousands of coloured bottles—he sat in the rotating chairs, and tried on a succession of wigs, grimacing at himself in the dusty mirrors. In an empty department-store he lost himself in a maze of furnished rooms, each like a stage-set, decorated in the styles of nearly half a century earlier. The synthetic curtain and carpet fabrics, with their elaborate patterns and lamé threads, were totally unlike the simple hand-woven worsteds and woollens of Garden City.

Halloway wandered around these darkened tableaux, these ghosts of bedroom suites and dining-rooms. He lay back grandly on an ornate four-poster, stroking the deep pile of the bedspread. What amused him, above all, was the feel of this vanished world, a surprise more tactile than visual.

In the dim light of a men's-wear department he pulled clothes racks on to the counters, jerked open the cabinet drawers. A cornucopia of suits and shirts, shoes and hats spilled across the floor. Stripping off his woollen trousers and jerkin, like the uniform of an ignorant medieval churl, he selected a new costume—red-white-and-blue sneakers, yellow suede trousers and a fleece-lined jacket with silver-thread embroidery and leather tassels as long as his arm.

In this modest attire he swung happily along the avenue. Thousands of cars lined the streets, their flamboyant bodywork covered with moss. Wild flowers peeped from the radiator grilles. Halloway stopped at every tenth car and tried to start the engine. Sitting behind these dead controls, he remembered the car he had found buried in the dunes at Garden City. The roof and doors had rusted away, but he sat for hours behind the wheel of this drowned hulk. By contrast, the cars here had barely been touched by the weather. Under the moss and dirt the lurid paint was as bright as ever.

Halloway was disappointed that none would start. Rocking a black limousine that took his fancy in an automobile showroom, he could hear the fuel still swishing in its tank.

'Somewhere, Halloway,' he told himself aloud, 'you'll find a car that runs. I've decided you're going to arrive in style ... '

At dusk, as Halloway passed a park filled with wild trees, shrubs and flowers of every kind, he realized that someone was following him. The soft tap of feet, sometimes barely moving, then running obliquely behind him, sounded faintly through the dark air. Heart racing, Halloway crouched among the cars. Nothing moved across the street. He filled his lungs with air, and broke away with a burst of speed, darting in and out of the cars. He dived through the open door of an evacuation bus parked by a hotel entrance and watched from the rear seats.

Five minutes later he saw the first of his shy pursuers. Edging forward cautiously, its eyes still on the park fifty yards away, a large deer hobbled along the sidewalk, searching the dim light for Halloway. Within moments two more appeared, steering their antlers through the overhead wires that trailed across the road.

As he watched them scenting the darkness, Halloway remembered the placid creatures in the zoo at Garden City, as lacking in aggression as these deer. The Angus and Hereford cows in their enclosure, the shire horses and saddleback pigs, the lambs, chicken and farmyard geese together memorialized all the vanished species of domestic animals. At Garden City everyone was vegetarian, not out of moral or religious conviction, but simply because they knew that the provision of grazing land, and the growing of cereal crops for animal feedstuffs, was a wastefully inefficient means of obtaining protein.

When the deer had gone, returning to their forest between the apartment blocks, Halloway stepped down from the bus. Knowing that he must spend the night somewhere, he walked up the steps into the hotel. On the seventh floor he found a bedroom from which he could see both the Sound and the skyscraper towers of the city centre. On the opposite shore the solar reflectors were still faintly visible, drinking in the last glow of the sunset, beacons of a vanished world. He slept through the night, dreaming of glass aeroplanes, their wings like mirrors, that circled the dark air over his head, waiting to carry him away to some sunlit eyrie among the clouds.

The next morning, after an early start, Halloway pressed on towards the city centre. He felt refreshed and confident again, fortified by an exotic breakfast of grapefruit juice, beans and peaches taken from the shelves of a near-by supermarket. Vaguely prudish about eating meat, he decided against opening any of the cans of pork and beef, the limitless varieties of salmon, tuna and sardine.

Bright sunlight filled the streets, picking out the vivid colours of the wild flowers growing in profusion from the cracked sidewalks. Despite these embellishments, the city's character had begun to change. Fastening his jacket across his chest, Halloway moved forward more cautiously. Above him, on all sides, were the massive structures and heavy technology of the late Twentieth Century – highway interchanges and bridge approaches, sixty-storey hotels and office-blocks. Between them, almost out of sight on the ground level, was a decaying under-stratum of bars and pin-table arcades, nightclubs and clothing stores. The cheap façades and neon signs had long since collapsed into the roads. A maze of narrow side-streets ran off in all directions, but by following only the main avenues he soon lost his bearings. A wide road raised on concrete stilts carried him high into the air, and changed course in a series of giant loops. Plodding around this curving viaduct, a cambered deck eight lanes wide, Halloway wasted nearly an hour in returning to his starting point.

It was at this time, shortly after he left the cloverleaf by an emergency staircase, that Halloway came across the first of the strange monuments he was later to find all over the city. As he stepped down from the pedestrian exit, he noticed that a nearby parking-lot had been used as a municipal dump. Old tyres, industrial waste and abandoned domestic appliances lay about in a rusty moraine. Rising from its centre was a pyramid of television sets some sixty feet high, constructed with considerable care and an advanced sense of geometry. The thousand or so sets were aligned shoulder to shoulder, their screens facing outwards, the combinations of different models forming decorative patterns on the stepped sides. The whole structure, from base to apex, was invaded by wild elders, moss and firethorn, the clouds of berries forming a huge cascade.

Halloway stared up at the rows of television sets, a pyramid of dead eyes in their worm-riddled cabinets, like the eggs of some voracious reptile waiting to be born from the bland globes embedded in this matrix of rotting organic matter. Pulled apart by the elders, many of the sets revealed their internal wiring. The green and yellow circuitry, the blue capacitors and modulators, mingled with the bright berries of the firethorn, rival orders of a wayward nature merging again after millions of years of separate evolution.

Little more than half a mile away, in a plaza between two office buildings, Halloway found a second pyramid. From a distance it resembled a funeral pyre of metal scrap built from hundreds of typewriters, telex machines and duplicators taken from the offices around the plaza, a monument to the generations of clerks and typists who had worked there. A series of narrow terraces rose one above the other, the tiers of typewriters forming ingenious baroque columns. Brilliant climbing plants, lobster-clawed clematis and honeysuckle with pink and yellow flowers, entwined themselves around the metal colonnades, the vivid blooms illuminating this memorial of rust.

Halloway mounted a staircase of filing cabinets to the upper terrace of the pyramid. On all sides, in the nearby streets and on the raised pedestrian areas above the plaza, an extraordinary vegetation had taken root. Dahlias, marigolds and cosmos flourished among the cracked paving-stones and in the ornamental urns outside the entrances to the office blocks. Along a three-hundred-yard section of the avenue all the cars had been cleared aside, and a field of poppies sprang from the broken asphalt. The bright, funereal flowers extended in a blood-red carpet down the line of hotels, as if waiting for a demonic visitor. Here and there an individual car had been picked out by this mysterious and profligate gardener, its windshield and windows knocked in and its cabin packed with blooms. As vivid as an explosion in a paint-shop, blue and carmine flowers and yellow-ribbed leaves crammed the open windows, mingled with tilting sunflowers and the vines that circled the roof and radiator grille.

From a side-street a quarter of a mile away came the sounds of collapsing masonry. Falling glass split the air. Halloway leapt down from the pyramid, holding to a column of typewriters as the road vibrated under his feet. The slow avalanche continued, the rumble of falling brick-work and the brittle ringing of breaking glass. Then Halloway heard the heavy beating of what he guessed was some kind of huge engine, throbbing with the same rhythm as the motor he had watched his father running in his workshop years before. It moved away, breaking through some glass and masonry obstruction in its path. Already the first dust was billowing from the end of the street, lit by thousands of coloured petals.

Halloway climbed into a nearby car, waiting as this machine moved away. In the deserted city the noise of the assault had carried with it an unmistakable violence, as if some huge and ugly creature was venting its anger at random on the buildings around it.

'Halloway, time to go ... ' Already he had decided to leave the city and make his way home. Once he had crossed the river he would be safe.

When the streets were quiet again, and the cloud of petalled dust had drifted away down the avenue, Halloway set off, leaving the monument of typewriters and telex machines behind him. He ran silently through the field of poppies, as the last petals fell through the unsettled air around him.

When he reached the side-street he found the roadway littered with human figures. Masonry and broken glass, sections of store window as large as his sailplane's wings, lay among the crushed flowers. Most of the clothing stores that lined both sides of this narrow street had been attacked, their glass fronts and window displays ripped out by some giant implement.

Everywhere the plastic mannequins lay in the sunlight, limbs crushed by the tracks of the machine, polite expressions looking up from the glass and masonry.

Frightened for the first time by the sight of violence, Halloway ran towards the river, and by luck found the open span of a large road-bridge that carried him away from the city. Without pausing to look back, ears listening for any sound of the machine, he sprinted along in his coloured sneakers. Half-way across the bridge he slowed down for the first time to catch his breath. The cloud of petals was still drifting eastwards between the office blocks. Halloway searched the northern suburbs for the mirror-sheathed building into which he had crashed, regretting that he would have to leave the sailplane among these anonymous streets patrolled by this violent machine.

Angry with himself, he pulled off his fleece-lined jacket and hurled it over the balustrade. It fell into the dead water like a sad, brilliant bird. Already he looked forward to his return to Garden City, with its civilized people and sane behaviour. Thinking back, his aggressiveness at the gliding championships embarrassed him.

'... too eager for action at any cost,' he reproved himself as he strode along. 'In future check that, Halloway ... '

He left the bridge and set off eastwards past the dockyards and warehouses. He had entered an area of single-storey factories and cheap housing, chemical tank-farms and electrical sub-stations. All around him, as well, were the monuments. He was crossing a plain of these memorials, pyramids of domestic appliances and car tyres, machine tools and office furniture that had been erected on any available patch of waste ground. Ignoring them, and their ambiguous flowers, Halloway pressed on. Already he could see the collapsed suspension bridge that marked the gateway to the Sound.

Shortly before noon, when the river crossing was three miles behind him, Halloway came across the airport. As he approached the perimeter fence he could see the control tower, and the tails of parked airliners as high as three-storey buildings. The entire surface of the airport, the concrete runways and grass verges, was covered with thousands of automobiles. Variants of no more than two or three models, they stretched away in a huge metallized dream.

Curious to see the airliners, Halloway followed the perimeter fence towards the entrance. He guessed that the cars had been new models fresh from the production line, stored here by the manufacturers when the oil tap had been turned off. With luck, one of the cars might start for him.

Now that he had left the city, Halloway began to relax again. The airport was a zone that he found curiously reassuring, and in some obscure way made up for the loss of his sailplane. He visualized his father landing and taking off in one of the single-engine aircraft parked nose-to-tail on the other side of the perimeter fence.

At the airport entrance, in the centre of a traffic island, Halloway found the largest of the pyramids he had seen so far. Well over one hundred feet high, the memorial had been constructed entirely from automobile radiator grilles, a tour-de-force of ironic humour. Row upon row, the grilles rose to the apex, cunningly welded together to form staircases and internal galleries. For once, the tropical flora had barely gained a purchase on the base of the pyramid, and the still-gleaming chrome formed a brilliant lacework.

Impressed by the structure, Halloway made his way around it into the airport. Service roads led in all directions to the terminal buildings and air-freight offices. Fuel tankers and breakdown vehicles blocked the narrow lanes. Losing himself in this maze, Halloway decided to climb to the roof of a ten-storey car-park whose canted floors spiralled up into the air behind the terminal buildings.

As he passed the elevators on his way to the staircase, Halloway without thinking touched the call button. To his surprise, the doors promptly responded, opening without any hesitation on well-oiled castors. The interior of the elevator was clean and well-maintained, the control panel freshly polished.

Listening to the faint drumming of an electric generator somewhere above the shaft, Halloway gathered his courage together. There was something seductive about this immaculate compartment, and already he was becoming impatient with himself for turning tail and leaving the city at the first alarm. Sooner or later he intended to come to terms with whatever creature prowled its deserted canyons, and this car-park would make a good observation post.

Stepping into the elevator, he inspected the control panel and pushed a button at random.

Within less than a minute he had ridden to the seventh

floor and stepped out into what he soon discovered was a museum of automobiles. At first glance the cars were indistinguishable from the thousands of vehicles he had passed that day. But as he walked through the dim light, seeing his reflection in the burnished cellulose and waxed leather, he realized that he had stumbled on to a unique private museum. The sixty or so cars on this canted deck were all exhibition pieces, sitting squarely on inflated tyres, antique coachwork lovingly restored.

'Pierce Arrow ... Bugatti ... Hispano-Suiza ... Chevrolet Impala ... ' Aloud, he read out the names from the manufacturers' medallions. Many of the cars dated back well over a century to the dawn of the automobile age, huge perambulators of brass and steel with high seats and coaching lamps larger than their diminutive engines. Others, slab-decked saloons and limousines, were as new as the models that covered the runways of the airport.

Cord. Stutz. Chrysler Imperial. Halloway climbed the deck to the eighth floor. More cars, all lovingly waxed and polished, faced each other through the gloom.

The one exception was parked in the centre of the ramp, a grimy six-wheeled breakdown truck with a heavy crane mounted on its rear platform. The engine cowling was still warm. Halloway opened the driver's door; on the seat were a toolkit and a set of maps of the city marked off into various zones. Ignition keys hung from the dashboard, and from the whole compartment came the raw but potent odour of carbonized oil, gasolene and engine coolant.

Sitting behind the steering wheel, Halloway felt the controls, trying to remember something of the casual expertise with which he so easily impressed the gang of ten-year-olds who watched him demonstrate how to drive.

Suddenly the engine was alive, thundering out between the concrete decks as if trying to shake itself apart. The heavy vehicle was vibrating fiercely, and the unlatched door bumped against Halloway's elbow. A blaze of lights lit up the dashboard. Gripping the wheel cautiously, Halloway released the handbrake and let the truck roll forward down the concrete incline, pressing the accelerator as the vehicle moved along at a steady two miles an hour.

Within thirty minutes he was driving around the airport at speed, roaring along the perimeter roads and down the one exposed section of runway. Flocks of startled ducks and geese rose from the reservoirs to the east of the airport, fleeing from the noise of the careening vehicle. When he first emerged from the car-park the truck had come to a halt, and it had taken Halloway some time to discover that the gear lever was in neutral. He soon learned to engage it, and set off at breakneck pace, slamming in and out of the parked cars. The heavy truck and its wildly swinging crane, steel hook lashing about, sent up a spray of rust from the cars kicked out of their way. The forward power of the vehicle, after the agile but passive motion of the sailplane, astonished Halloway. The slightest pressure of his foot on the accelerator sent the truck hurtling ahead. It was the raw energy of the machine that most impressed him, this gut-driven dynamo totally at one with the city across the river.

Carried away by his new-found determination, and confident that he could take on any opponent now, Halloway headed out of the airport. As he left the main gates he was already moving at sixty m.p.h. Too late, he released the accelerator as the road veered off to circle the traffic island with its pyramid of radiator grilles. Trying to slow down, he plunged across the grass verge, the concrete kerb almost rolling the truck on to its side. It hurtled forward, the crane's hook and heavy chains thrashing the cabin behind Halloway's head. He clung to the wheel, face hidden behind his arms, and felt himself flung across the cabin as the truck struck the lowest tier of the pyramid. It tore out a dozen radiator grilles, which hung like trophies from the dented fenders as it swerved away, ran head-on into the steel pylon of a route indicator and came to a halt on its side, cabin buried in the soft earth.

He was waking from a dream of powered flight.

He soared across a dark, windless sky. Through the rigging and fuselage struts behind his head came the steady beat of an engine. Beside him in the cockpit a man was crouching over the controls, as if hiding himself from Halloway. When he tried to see the face of this mysterious pilot the aircraft banked steeply, throwing Halloway against the canopy. Searching for a way to escape from the aircraft, he realized that it was built of glass, and that he could see the stars through the wings and fuselage. Unable to restrain himself, he seized the man's shoulder and tried to wrest the control column from him. As they struggled together the aircraft plunged across the sky, its engine screaming ...

He woke to find himself in a dimly lit cabin, lying on a bed attached to the panelled wall. Leaning over Halloway, pulling with concern at his shoulder, was a young man about five years older than himself, a tall, slimly built Negro with an expression of wary concern on his shy but intelligent face.

Rest—you've landed safely.

A line of scarlet letters, in a stylized computer typeface, glowed in Halloway's eyes, hovering in the air two feet from him.

Can you hear me? You're not flying now.

Halloway nodded weakly, gazing at the messages that seemed to emerge from the man's hand. Although there were windows in the cabin the air outside was almost opaque, as if they were contained by yet another building. Twenty feet away a second ceiling tilted across the sky.

'There was an engine on the glider,' Halloway explained. He sat up, pointing to the roof of the cabin. Somewhere above him there was the steady drumming of an internal-combustion engine. 'I can hear it now ... '

Lights flickered in the Negro's palm. Again the strange alphabet sorted itself into a message. His pensive eyes presided over these reassembling letters as if over the anagrams of stigmata.

There is a power generator on the roof.

As if to reassure Halloway, he pressed a wall switch.

When the electric light – an antique tungsten-filament glow – came on in the cabin Halloway examined his surroundings. He was lying on a bunk in a large land-cruiser, one of a group drawn up together on what he guessed was the top floor of the car-park. In front of him, beyond a small kitchen, was the driver's compartment, the steering wheel and instrument panel below a high windshield.

Sitting beside him, clearly relieved to see Halloway regain consciousness, was the tenant of the cruiser. The left side of his face was covered by a fretwork of notches, minute cuts clearly inflicted during his childhood. At first Halloway assumed that they were some kind of tribal insignia, but later he learned that they were the scars left by a serious automobile accident.

With his intelligent face and curiously unfocused eyes, which seemed to be fixed on some point within his mind, he reminded Halloway of a circus clown without his make-up. He sat here in his land-cruiser with the same vaguely melancholy posture of the clowns whom Halloway and his friends visited in their trailers whenever they toured Garden City. As he gazed down at Halloway with his alert but neutral expression he looked as if he had been alone too long, and was unsure how to respond to the physical presence of another human being.

He touched Halloway's shoulder, obviously convincing himself that his visitor posed no threat.

Now – are you all right?

'I'm a lot better. I guess it was your truck I crashed.'

His rescuer waved this aside. He seemed about to speak, but checked himself. In one hand, almost hidden between his slim fingers, was a pocket calculator. With surprising swiftness, he tapped out a message, which flashed up on the alphanumeric display.

Forget it. There's not exactly a shortage here.

As he gazed through the window of the cruiser Halloway had the distinct impression that this solitary young mute was a prisoner here, high above this museum of cars in the centre of the abandoned airport. His fingers fluttered across the keys of the calculator. As each sentence came up it was glanced at and quickly erased, fingers flicking away in this reverse Braille. Obviously he was used to holding long conversations with himself.

'I'm sorry about the truck,' Halloway said. Remembering the frightening violence he had witnessed that morning, he asked cautiously: 'Do you live here? What's your name?'

Olds.

'Olds? What, as in—?' Halloway laughed, despite himself, but the young Negro nodded, clearly taking no offence. Joining in the joke, he touched the scars on his scalp. Fingers flicked across the keyboard.

Yes. As in Oldsmobile. Ten years ago I renamed myself.

He stared at the illuminated message, his mind drifting away. An expression of regret hovered around his faint smile.

'Why not?' Halloway said encouragingly. 'I like it, it's a good name.' He looked at his watch. It was after two o'clock. He felt drawn to this solitary young Negro, but it was time to be moving on.

'Olds, I ought to be going.'

All right. But first have some food.

They left the cabin and stepped down on to the tenth floor of the car-park. Four of the land-cruisers were drawn up to form a private enclosure. From the balustrade Halloway looked down at the thousands of vehicles that covered the airport.

The breakdown truck lay on its side by the pyramid of radiator grilles. He took for granted that Olds had constructed these monuments. On trestle tables beside the land-cruisers lay an extensive selection of electrical parts – dynamos and transformers, fuse-boxes and switching units. Power cables trailed across the floor, running from the generator on the roof to a barbecue in the centre of what he assumed was Olds' dining area. Rotating on the spit was the body of a small deer. The fused flesh gleamed like polished oak. Olds beckoned Halloway to a chair, and began to cut steaks from the carcass.

An hour later Halloway had finished the most intoxicating meal of his life, and made his decision to postpone any return to Garden City for as long as possible. After the pallid vegetarian cuisine of his childhood, the flavour of venison and animal fat acted on him like adrenaline. Surrounded by the bones and meat scraps, he felt like the early pioneers who had colonized this land and built its cities.

Olds had watched him eat with obvious pleasure. At intervals, as he urged him to take second and third helpings, his right hand flicked out some brief message to himself on the calculator, as if he were transcribing a commentary on a second life going on inside his head.

During their meal he told Halloway about himself, and how as a boy of five years old during the final evacuation of the city he had been knocked down by a housewife driving her Oldsmobile to the neighbourhood scrap-yard. Thus he had become the world's last traffic casualty. Fifteen years later, after a long and incomplete recovery from his brain injuries, he left the technical training centre at the commune hospital fifty miles to the north of the city and made his home among the thousands of cars parked on the runways of this abandoned airport. Here, moved by some profound compulsion, he spent his time putting together this museum of cars, perhaps in an attempt to find the missing sections of his mind. His ambition, he explained to Halloway, was to have a running model of every make of car ever manufactured.

Only then will I come to terms with my accident.

He flashed a self-deprecating smile and added:

After that I can learn to fly.

Halloway nodded sympathetically, unsure whether Olds was pulling his leg. This clever, shy but self-confident man seemed to be all there as far as Halloway could tell. When they had finished the meal Halloway asked Olds to take him on a tour of the museum.

'You repaired all these yourself? It's hard to believe – in the first place, what about the fuel?'

Olds gestured casually at the sea of vehicles that stretched to the horizon on all sides of the car-park.

There are five million cars in this city alone. Almost every tank still has a little gas in it.

Halloway walked down the line of cars, gazing at his reflections in the lovingly refurbished radiator grilles, hub-caps and chromium trim. Olds led the way, pointing out a rare Mercedes 600, a Rolls-Royce Silver Cloud, a Facel Vega. He was clearly proud to show off his collection, but at the same time Halloway noticed that he seemed slightly bored by these vehicles. His eyes were forever straying to the moss-covered airliners parked by the terminal buildings.

'And you're sure they all run?' Halloway asked. He pointed to a resplendant limousine. 'What about this one – Daimler Majestic?'

With remarkable speed, Olds leapt behind the wheel of the car. Within seconds its engine roared out, headlamps pulsed, momentarily blinding Halloway. The horn sounded imperiously.

'Olds, it's unbelievable!' Halloway congratulated him. 'Let's see you try another – this Pontiac Firebird.'

For the next thirty minutes the two men moved

through the museum, Halloway shouting and pointing to one car after another, Olds leaping like an excited faun, an automotive Ariel, from one driver's seat to the next, switching on the ignitions and bringing the engines to life. Each car he left with its motor racing and headlamps full on. First a dozen cars came alive, then more than thirty, and finally the entire eighth and ninth decks of the car-park. The roar of the engines, the exhaust swirling in the headlamp beams, the vibrating floors and balustrades, the smell of burning fuel and the noise booming out over the deserted airport, made Halloway feel that the entire city had begun to spring to life, re-starting itself under the hands of this young recluse.

Finally, out of curiosity rather than cruelty, Halloway shouted out the last name. 'One more, Olds! What about –' In the absence of the car, he pointed at random. '– Oldsmobile!'

Immediately Halloway regretted the prank. Too late, he saw the rictus on Olds' face. Sitting behind the wheel of a white Galaxie, he began to pound the controls, angry with the car when it failed to start on its own. When Halloway reached him he had slumped back and was already moving into a deep fugue, mouth agape, the blood in his face making a livid lace-work of the scars. On the seat beside him, like some hyper-excited small animal, his right hand flicked out a desperate message on the calculator.

'Olds ... it doesn't matter!'

Halloway pulled open the door and tried to calm him. Bizarre messages glimmered among the headlamps as he sank into unconsciousness, the engines of a hundred cars throbbing around him in the exhaust-filled air.

Teach me to fly!

Within an hour Olds had recovered. Sitting back on a car seat beside the barbecue, he touched his face and scalp, feeling the tracery of scars as if making sure that the jigsaw was once again in place. After dragging him to the elevator and taking him back to his lair, Halloway had moved among the cars, switching off the engines one by one. When the building was silent again he leaned against the balustrade, looking out at the distant towers of the city. Despite the moss-covered airliners by the terminal buildings, Halloway noticed that he was no longer thinking of his quest for his parents' apartment. Already the elements of a far grander scheme were forming in his mind.

They sat together in the dusk, listening to the steady beat of the generator on the roof, their faces lit by the glow of the barbecue.

With the same innocent guile that he used on his grandfather, Halloway said: 'Olds, you're a genius with cars. But can you start up anything else?'

Olds nodded soberly at Halloway, not taken in by him for a moment. He inspected his slim hands, as if resigned to the talents multiplying from his fingertips.

Anything. I can make anything work.

'I believe you, Olds. We'll find my sailplane and you can put an engine and propeller on it. Then I'll teach you how to fly.'

Early the next morning Olds and Halloway set off together from the airport. Olds selected, apparently at random, another breakdown vehicle from his stable of trucks and pick-ups on the first floor of the car-park. Into the rear section, where a generator was bolted to the deck, he slung a leather tool-case and reels of power cable. He had recovered from his seizure of the previous afternoon. Something about the prospect of flying had given him back his self-confidence. As they left the airport, circling the pyramid of radiator grilles, he flicked a series of questions at Halloway.

What engine size? How many horse-power?

'I can't remember,' Halloway admitted. Already he

was having to pretend that he had flown a powered craft. 'Big enough to drive a propeller. The size of this truck's?'

Far too heavy. I'll find an aero-engine.

They crossed the river and headed northwards through the city. At intervals Olds would check his fuel gauge, stop the truck in the centre of the street and leap out with a siphon hose. He moved around, shaking the parked cars and listening to the swish of fuel.

Once, while Olds was sucking away at his hose, Halloway strolled across the sidewalk to a small bar. A juke-box stood in the doorway, thick dust covering the extravagant plastic front. Halloway pressed the buttons at random, and then wandered off along the street.

When he returned five minutes later Olds had disappeared. The truck stood in the roadway, the engine of the power generator ticking over smoothly. The tool-bag had gone, and cables ran from the generator across the sidewalk.

'Olds! Let's go!'

Then he heard music coming from the bar. There was a jangle of coarse sound, a rapid beat of drums and guitars, and a rock-and-roll singer's voice bellowed across the empty street.

When he reached the bar he found Olds crouched behind the juke-box, tool-kit open on the floor. Like a leather carpet-bag fitted with hundreds of pockets, it seemed to contain every tool ever devised. Olds' arms were deep inside the entrails of the machine, hooking up a series of extension leads to a transformer.

When Halloway put his hands to his ears Olds switched off. He winked at Halloway.

That's only a beginning.

He was as good as his word. As they pressed on down the endless avenues lined with office-blocks, hotels and department-stores, Olds would stop the truck, seize his tool-kit and unwind his cables across the street. In rapid succession he started up three pin-tables in an amusement arcade, a line of washing machines in a launderette, a telex and two ticker-tapes in the ground-floor office of a commercial business, and a complete appliance range in a home equipment store. As if in rehearsal for some lunatic household, mixers whirred, fan-heaters pumped, vacuum cleaners roared, a dozen other gadgets clattered and whistled.

Watching all this, Halloway was impressed by the casual way Olds turned on these devices. They moved northwards, animating these minuscule portions of the city, leaving behind them these happy nodes of activity.

Confused by the noise and excitement, Halloway sat limply in the truck when they reached the mirror-sheathed office block into which he had crashed. The sailplane lay among the cars, its broken wings stirring in the light air. As Olds moved around it, inspecting the inverted cockpit with his gentle but shrewd eyes, Halloway half-expected him to reassemble the glider with a few waves of his screwdriver.

Olds pointed to the humpbacked cockpit, where the strengthened fuselage frame behind the pilot's seat formed a platform whose purpose Halloway had never understood.

This is a real aircraft. Designed to take an engine. But you built it to look like a glider?

'I know,' Halloway lied. 'I couldn't find the right power-plant.'

Olds' quick hands were exploring the interior of the fuselage.

Runs for control lines. A fuel-tank compartment. It's well thought out. And room for both of us.

'What?' Genuinely surprised, Halloway peered into the cockpit.

Behind the pilot's bulkhead there's space for a passenger.

As Olds pointed with the calculator, Halloway stared at what his father clearly designed to be a rear seat. Had his mother and father planned to leave him behind when they flew off? Or perhaps his father had intended to take his son with him, the two of them soaring back to the city together. Puzzled by these discoveries, he noticed Olds watching him in a shrewd but still kindly way. Did Olds really believe that Halloway had designed this powered glider himself? Was he using Halloway in exactly the same way that Halloway was trying to exploit him?

For the time being it hardly mattered. Halloway took the wheel for the return journey to the airport, after they dismantled the glider and lashed the sections to the truck. The power and noise of the engine erased all doubts. Barely controlling his excitement, he tried to hold down their speed as they raced through the streets.

'Olds! Watch this!'

They crossed a section of the roadway planted with poppies, the vivid but sinister flowers extending in front of them for three hundred yards. The bumper of the truck scythed through the flowers, and a dense cloud of petals billowed into the air, staining the sky like a miniature sunset. Halloway turned and made a second run through the poppies, almost standing at the wheel as they hurtled through the whirling petals.

As they approached the centre of the city Halloway drove around the side-streets, hunting out any other of these floral tracts planted here in the broken asphalt by some aberrant gardener. Soon millions of leaves were drifting through the coloured air. There were white streets where they found daisies, yellow avenues filled with a mist of crushed buttercups, blue boulevards which wept a rain of forget-me-nots.

Then, as they emerged from a storm of daffodil petals, Halloway nearly collided into a large industrial tractor moving along the roadway in front of him. Pulling to a halt behind its high rear assembly, he flung Olds on to the dashboard. Halloway switched off the engine, and watched this massive tracked vehicle lumbering slowly through the haze of petals. A hydraulic ram was mounted in front of the motor, fitted with an immense claw that now held a single automobile, carried in the air fifteen feet from the ground.

In the control cabin a dark-haired man in a black plastic jacket emblazoned with silver studs was operating the steering levers. His face was barely visible through the whirling petals, and he seemed unaware of the truck stalled behind him. However, when Halloway restarted his engine, intending to overtake the tractor, the driver swung his claw to the right, blocking Halloway with the swinging automobile. Looking up at the man's handsome face, with its hard mouth like a piece of gristle, Halloway was certain that it was this driver, and this terrifying machine, which had destroyed the garment store mannequins the previous day.

Halloway began to reverse the truck down the street, but Olds held his arm warningly.

Follow him. Stillman needs to be given his own way.

As Halloway moved forward, following the tractor, Olds sat back. He had switched off the calculator, and seemed to have forgotten their exhilarating race through the flowers, his mind moving elsewhere, bored by the prospect of whatever was to come.

They emerged into an open square, set in the heart of one of the oldest sections of the city, an area of theatres, bars and cheap hotels. Rising from the centre of the square was the largest of the eccentric memorials to Twentieth-Century technology that Halloway had seen so far. At first glance it resembled a gothic cathedral, built entirely from rusting iron, glass and chromium. As they crossed the square, following the tractor, Halloway realized that this structure was built entirely from the bodies of automobiles. Stacked one upon the other, they formed a palisade of towers that rose two hundred feet into the air.

A group of heavy cranes and a buttress of scaffolding

marked out the working face, overlooked by an observation platform reached by a simple elevator. Standing at the rail, and waiting for the tractor to carry its latest contribution to the memorial, was a small, pugnacious man of advanced age. Although well into his eighties, he was dressed like a physical education instructor in immaculate white sweater and well-creased trousers. Inspecting Halloway's glider with a critical eye, he picked up an electric megaphone and began to call out instructions in a high voice to the driver of the tractor.

Olds was gazing up at the monument of cars, shaking his head as if ruefully aware that he and this odd old man were in the same business. He switched on the calculator.

I'll wait for you here. You're about to meet Mr Buckmaster. Viceroy, czar, and warden of this island.

Halloway waited as the driver climbed down from his cab. Deliberately taking his time, he sauntered over to Halloway, pointing to his red, white and blue sneakers, yellow trousers and shirt covered with petals.

'The Rainbow Kid – you come down from the sky and have yourself a time ... '

Although twice Halloway's age, with slicked-back hair and a pale skin that would always appear dirty, he had a lazy, youthful aura, as if a large section of his life had passed in his absence and he himself had never aged beyond his twenties. For all his sarcastic manner, he seemed watchful and ready to ingratiate himself at a moment's notice. With his self-directed aggression and stylized swagger he was a type Halloway had never known at Garden City, but which all his reading confirmed was a classic specimen of metropolitan man.

'Take the elevator,' he told Halloway. 'Mr Buckmaster has been waiting to meet you. He'll want to induct you into his work-force.'

'This monument – and the others? He built them all?'

'*I* built them. Buckmaster merely dreamed up the whole mad idea. Homage to the Chrysler Corporation,

Datsun and General Motors. When we've finished, the spirit of Karl Benz will be laid to rest under a million driver's licences and parking tickets.'

He slammed the elevator grille in Halloway's face and punched the ascend button.

The old man in his whites was waiting for Halloway when he reached the observation platform. On a card-table lay a set of blueprints, and Halloway could see that if ever completed the structure would rise some four hundred feet into the air.

The old man beckoned Halloway to the rail. Everything about him, his quick eyes and mouth, his restless hands, was in a hurry. He talked to Halloway as if he had known him for years and was resuming a conversation interrupted only a few seconds earlier.

'It looks a mess, eh? Just a pile of automobiles, a million junkyards are full of them. What do I think I'm doing? Wait and see.' He pointed to Halloway's glider on the back of the truck, where Olds was already tearing away the torn fabric. 'Is that a glider or a power-plane? During the war I built thirty thousand fighters for the government, we were turning them out so fast the Air Force kept the war going just to get rid of them. And that was on top of a hundred airships, cargo-submarines and enough spare parts to give every man on this planet his own robot-assembly kit. Then I re-tooled and flooded the world with wrist-watch TVs, compressed paper houses, a million gimmicks. Techniques of mass production raised to the nth power. Do you remember my protein synthesizer?' He glanced at Halloway, who nodded promptly. 'No, you're too young. No bigger than a suitcase, you put it under your bed at night and it ran off your sweat and body temperature. Somehow it didn't catch on, but I would have fed a starving world, lifted the population of this planet to fifty billion in comfort. I was ready to build them super-cities, the first conurbation conglomerates, the mega-metropolis larger than any individual nation-state. I designed the first collapsible city, interchangeable parts moving around on gigantic rails. Makes sense – if a theatre isn't being used by day, wheel it off and roll on an office-block. Instead of which' – here he raised his ancient hands eloquently to the empty streets – 'they all just gave up and faded away. Goodbye, C20 Man, hello Arcadia, that timid world of water wheels and solar batteries. Not that there's an unlimited future for tidal power. Every time one of those pontoons nods its head the planet slows down a little. The days are getting longer ... '

He turned away from the rail, and put a hard arm around Halloway's shoulder. 'Now, you've come to work for me? It's too late, I closed down my last design office ten years ago.' He steered Halloway to the elevator, nodding sagely to himself as they rode down together. 'A pity, you could have done great things with those hands. Anyway, you can work for Stillman, there's more than he can do.'

'Well ... ' Halloway glanced at the black-jacketed driver, standing beside the tractor with one hand on the automobile suspended in the air over his head. 'I was thinking of setting up on my own.'

'Good for you – but it's all over. There's nothing to do now but close it down. Give it a humane burial, put up a monument here and there to Twentieth-Century technology, to all those things we took for granted – tyres, engines, TVs, kitchen appliances, automobiles ... '

His voice wavered for the first time and then stopped, as he gazed up wistfully at his cathedral of cars. Waiting for this strange old man to start again, Halloway remembered that he had seen his combative jaw and dreamer's eyes in the architecture textbooks in his grandfather's library. Buckmaster had been the last of the great entrepreneur-industrialists, part architect and engineer, part visionary, driven on by old-fashioned crankiness, ceaseless originality and a well-developed talent for seizing the headlines. Grandiose projects started all over the world and then abandoned to rivals and pupils, a succession of wives, the third of whom died in a mysterious scandal, lawsuits against any number of governments, plans for the first trans-Atlantic bridge—these were elements in a stormy career spanning nearly seventy years. Although Buckmaster was clearly living a century too late there was something about his unflagging energy and resolve that fired a response in Halloway's mind. He couldn't help contrasting Buckmaster's limitless appetite for steel, power, concrete and raw materials with the self-denying, defeatist lives of the engineers and architects at Garden City. There was even a fringe group of scientific fanatics—the so-called 'heliophiles'—whose ambition was to return energy to the sun by firing off all the old missiles with nuclear warheads, repaying the sun for its billion-year bounty.

He followed Buckmaster into the interior of the memorial, uneasily aware that this cathedral of rust might collapse at any time. At the far end of the nave the semi-circle of internal walls had been transformed into a lavish botanical garden. Terrace upon terrace of climbing plants hung from the chassis of the cars, brilliant flowers bloomed in the windows and wheel-wells. The golden bells of forsythia trailed from the windows of grand limousines a hundred feet in the air, the white mist of mile-a-minute vines hovered like steam above the radiator grilles and exhaust pipes.

Apparently unaware that this cascade of blossoms was already transforming his monument into a far more bizarre structure than he had visualized, Buckmaster began to point out various details of the construction. But Halloway was more interested in the hanging garden. A young woman was working at the flowers, taking nasturtium and petunia seedlings from a series of trays and planting them in the doors and windows. As she moved about, climbing up and down a high ladder, Halloway had difficulty in guessing her age. At Garden City the emancipated women wore simple home-woven smocks and jerkins indistinguishable from the men's. With undressed hair and devoid of make-up, their sexual roles were always explicit, desire worn casually on their sleeves.

By contrast, this young woman – his daughter Miranda, Buckmaster informed him – was dressed like the heroine of a lavishly costumed period musical. Everything about her, from her extravagant copper-tinted hair in a Pre-Raphaelite cut to her long white neck and embroidered art-nouveau gown, was calculated for concealment and effect, artifice and allure. Later, Halloway discovered that she changed her appearance every day, moving through the deserted boutiques and fashion-houses of the city, modelling herself on the vanished styles of the Twentieth Century. On one day she would appear in a cream cloche hat and Gatsby gown, on another in a lurex blouse, bobby sox and teenager's flared tartan skirt.

Buckmaster introduced Halloway to her. 'Miranda, a new recruit – Mr Halloway, an aviator from Garden City. Any more like him and I may have to think again about opening my design office.'

As the old man wandered around, nodding at the profusion of flowers, Halloway searched for something to say. In his yellow trousers and multi-coloured sneakers he was as much in costume as Buckmaster's daughter, but he felt gauche and clumsy beside her. Although she was his own age, there was something naive, and at the same time knowing and sophisticated, about Miranda. He guessed that he was the first young man of eighteen she had met, but that she had done a great deal of thinking about the subject and for all her shyness was well prepared to deal with him on her own terms.

'We watched you driving around,' she told him matter-of-factly and without any rancour. 'Killing all those flowers – in a way it must have been fun.'

'Well ... ' Lamely, Halloway tried to apologize. He helped her down the ladder, relieved when she was on his own level. There was something unsettling about the way she had looked down at him, surrounded by the vine-infested cars. 'I didn't realize that they were yours. I'll help you to plant them again – they'll soon grow.'

'I know.' She strolled around him, picking the petals from his shirt, as if removing spots of blood. 'Sometimes I feel like the daughter of some great magician – wherever I touch, a flower springs up.'

Halloway brushed away the last of the petals. His difficulty in talking to her stemmed partly from her ambiguity, the naively teasing sexual come-on, but more from his own inexperience. In Garden City the relations between young people were governed by the most enlightened rules, derived from the teachings of Malinowski, Margaret Mead and the anthropologists who had followed them. From the age of sixteen, in the approved Polynesian style, young people of both sexes lived together openly in the 'long house' dormitories set aside for them until they later chose their marriage partner. Halloway had opted out of this, for reasons he had never understood, so committing himself to the company of his grandparents on one side and the younger teenagers on the other. He had never regretted the decision – there was something far too amiable, far too bovine and uncritical, about the hand-holding tenants of the long house.

Now, as he watched Miranda admiring his coloured sneakers, swirling her embroidered dress around him, he was certain that he was right. That ambiguity she showed, that moody combination of challenge and allure, was exactly what the city was about.

'I saw your glider yesterday,' Miranda told him. 'Crossing the Sound. It was like part of a dream, miles away across the water. Now suddenly you're here, in your miracle shoes.'

'*I* dream about powered flight,' Halloway told her with

some pride. 'Olds and I are rebuilding the glider. When it's ready we'll put an engine on it.'

Miranda nodded, gazing up at her hanging garden, as if waiting patiently for the jungle to return. In some way she seemed almost at odds with her father, trying to undo his work and transform it for her own purposes.

'Halloway ... ' She touched his arm. 'My father's very old. I want him to finish this before it's too late. Stillman's losing interest. Will you work for us for a while?'

The next day Halloway joined Stillman's one-man construction gang. He had said goodbye to Olds, who returned with the sailplane to the airport, and spent the night in one of the small hotels around the square.

Riding on the cowling of the tractor's engine, Halloway squatted in front of the driving cab as Stillman roved the city, searching for the exact models of the cars that Buckmaster had ordered. Each one they carried back to the monument, and Halloway climbed the wall of vehicles and guided Stillman as he steered the largest of the cranes and inserted the car into its place. From the observation platform the old industrialist supervised the work from behind his blueprints. Meanwhile his daughter, dressed for the day in a 1940s business suit, with boxy shoulders and a skirt of brown pin-stripe, her hair in a frizz, moved silently among the flowers in the centre of the memorial, tending the vines and blossoms in this dark, humid arbour.

His involvement with this strange trio surprised Halloway, but he soon realized that each of them played a role in certain unfolding obsessions of his own. Of the three, Stillman with his black jacket and hoodlum style most disturbed and most stimulated him, brooding over a dark dream of the city so like Halloway's own.

As they drove back through the streets on that first day Halloway had an unsettling glimpse of Stillman's unpredictable violence. The massive tractor was clanking down a wide avenue, a yellow taxi-cab held in its claw, when they passed a department store. Halloway was sitting in front of the cab, and was nearly flung to the road as Stillman slammed back the left-hand drive lever and turned the tractor towards the sidewalk. Cars were parked nose to tail along the kerb, but Stillman drove straight into them, knocking them out of his way with powerful left and right swings of the taxi. Gripped by the claw, the battered vehicle showered glass and rust on to the road. Working the levers and throttle with hard and almost spasm-like thrusts of his arms and shoulders, Stillman drove the tractor towards the store. His jaws champed rapidly on a piece of gum, but his face was deliberately expressionless, part of a continuous stylization of gesture and movement that Halloway had never seen before and that excited and disturbed him at the same time.

A group of mannequins sat in the store window around a table, part of a mock dinner-party that had started twenty-five years earlier and never proceeded beyond the waxy hors d'œuvres. The polite poses and prim over-elegant manners clearly pulled a hair-trigger in Stillman's mind. As the plate glass collapsed into the sidewalk he slung aside the taxi, sending it rolling across the street, and then began to sweep the mannequins out of the window, scattering them on to the sidewalk.

As he watched the destruction of these smartly attired female figures, Halloway was thinking of Miranda and her obsessive changes of costume. Was this her way of containing Stillman, or of provoking him? Stillman stared at her with a kind of humourless irony, as if forming in his mind a series of obscene jokes about her. Only his deference to the old industrialist seemed to prevent him from assaulting Miranda.

Seizing the yellow taxi again, Stillman set off down the street, the shattered mannequins lying in their tailored rags like the well-to-do victims of a terrorist attack in a fashionable shopping centre. Halloway was shaking with excitement, barely able to keep his seat on the engine cowling. For all his fear of Stillman, he knew that he was half-hoping that he would be violent again. He imagined the city filled with people, their lives invigorated by just this kind of callous and stylized aggression. When they passed another clothing store with a group of mannequins in the window he tapped the windshield and pointed them out to Stillman.

Later, when Buckmaster and his daughter retired to their third-floor suite in a hotel facing the monument of cars, Stillman and Halloway wandered through the dusk towards a nearby park. Stillman broke into a gunshop, and from the racks behind the counter took down a sporting rifle and shotgun. Pockets filled with cartridges, they strolled into the park, and in the evening light shot quail and a small deer. The roar of gunfire, the coarse smell of the cordite and the hard recoil against his arms and shoulders, the terrified movement of thousands of birds and animals as they fled through the forest, together filled Halloway's head with fantasies of violence.

Stillman occupied a penthouse apartment on the twentieth floor of a block facing the park.

'It's a long climb,' he warned Halloway. 'But I like to sit up there in the morning and watch dinner grazing down below.'

On the open terrace they lit a fire with pieces of furniture taken from the other apartments. Around them the walls of the city rose into the night. As he roasted the quail and turned the deer on its spit Halloway could see the flames reflected in thousands of darkened windows, as if the night were on fire. They sat together in armchairs by the embers flaring in the wind, and Stillman talked about the city, of the period he could just remember when it had been filled with more than a million people, the streets packed with traffic and the skies with helicopters, a realm of ceaseless noise and activity, competition and crime. It was here, in fact, as a young student at the school of architecture, that Stillman had first met Buckmaster. Within six months he had killed the industrialist's third wife in a lovers' quarrel. The last murderer to be tried and convicted before the emigration from the cities began in earnest, he was sentenced to twenty years' imprisonment. Eighteen years later, rotting away in an empty penitentiary, the sole prisoner looked after by one aged warder, he had been freed by Buckmaster, who took him on his own parole in a strange gesture. Now he worked for the old man, operating the heavy lifting equipment and helping him to build his monuments to a vanished age of technology. All the while he could barely contain his anger at finding the city he had longed for through so many years an empty and abandoned shell.

Halloway listened to him without speaking. When Stillman finished and lay back in his armchair, staring at the embers of the fire and the bones scattered at his feet, Halloway walked to the balustrade and looked at the dark buildings around them.

'Stillman – it isn't too late. It's all waiting for us here. We can start it up again. Olds can bring it back to life for us.'

During the next month, as he continued to work for the old industrialist on his memorials, Halloway began his self-appointed task of reanimating this huge metropolis. The cathedral of cars now reached to a height of three hundred feet, an eccentric but impressive structure of steel, glass and chrome. As it neared completion Buckmaster began to slow down, as if aware that this last monument would mark the end of his life and career.

Free during the afternoons, Halloway returned to Stillman's apartment house. Invariably he found the slim patient figure of Olds standing beside his breakdown truck. The mute's hopes of learning to fly, his dream of escape from the thousands of cars that surrounded him at the airport and the memories of his accident, had become the central obsession of his life. On the one afternoon when Halloway could spare the time to visit the airport he found his sailplane on the roof of the car park, tethered to the sloping concrete deck like a prisoner of the sky. Olds had rebuilt the wings and fuselage, and was already preparing a fifty horse-power engine and propeller to be mounted above the cockpit.

Nodding his approval, Halloway noticed that the museum of cars was already showing signs of neglect. Dust filmed the once immaculate coachwork, leaves and tags of paper lay against the unwiped windshields. As Olds gazed at the sailplane the calculator in his hand flickered continuously.

Halloway, we'll leave soon. When I've assembled the engine.

'Of course,' Halloway reassured him. 'We're going together, I know.'

Flying lessons?

There was panic in the quivering letters.

I can't fly yet!

'Olds, naturally. You won't find it difficult – look at the way you handle machinery, you're a genius.'

But Olds was only interested in the aircraft. In the aviation section of one of the city's science museums he found a leather flying suit and helmet dating back to World War I. He took to wearing the costume, his slight figure and scarred head encased in this antique aviator's gear.

For the time being, Halloway decided to humour him. Olds was essential to his plan to restart the city, and without his electrical and mechanical skills the metropolis would remain as dead as a tomb. In return for the promise of flying lessons, Olds drove in from the airport each afternoon, equipped with his generators, cables and tool-kit.

Sceptical of Halloway's ambitious scheme, Stillman wandered through the densely forested park with his rifle, killing the birds. Meanwhile Olds fitted the apartment house with its own electricity supply. A gasolene-driven generator in the entrance hall was soon pounding away, its power supply plugged into the mains. Even this small step immediately brought the building alive. Halloway moved from one apartment to the next, flicking lights on and off, working the appliances in the kitchens. Mixers chattered, toasters and refrigerators hummed, warning lights glowed in control panels. Most of the equipment, barely used during the long period of power cuts twenty-five years earlier, was still in functioning order. Television sets came on, radios emitted a ghostly tonelessness interrupted now and then by static from the remote-controlled switching units of the tidal pumps twenty miles away along the Sound.

However, in the tape-recorders, stereo-systems and telephone answering machines Halloway at last found the noise he needed to break the silence of the city. At first, playing through these tapes of conversations recorded by husbands and wives in the last years of the Twentieth Century, Halloway was disturbed by the anxious queries and despairing messages that described the slow collapse of an entire world. The sense of gloom and psychic entropy that came through these reminders to queue for gasolene and cooking oil were the absolute opposite of the vigour and dynamism he had expected.

But the music was different. Almost every apartment seemed to be a broadcasting station of its own. Bursting with crude confidence, the music transformed these ghost-filled rooms into a battery of nightclubs. He moved from floor to floor, blowing the dust from records and cassettes, switching on each of the apartments in turn. Rock-and-roll, big band, jazz and pop boomed through the open windows at the silent park. Even Stillman was impressed, looking up in surprise from the waist-high grass, shotgun raised hesitantly to the air as if thinking twice about trying to make an equal noise.

'Olds, it works!' Halloway found him resting by the generator in the lobby. 'If we can switch on this building we can switch on the whole city! Take off that flying cap and we'll start now.'

Reluctantly, Olds peeled off his helmet. He smiled ungrudgingly at Halloway, clearly admiring the energy and enthusiasm of this excited young man, but at the same time he seemed to be estimating his degree of involvement with Halloway. Although surrounded by his tools and cables, ammeters and transformers, his mind was clearly miles away, in the cockpit of the glider on the roof of the car-park. He looked bored by what he was doing, hardly the mechanic to the world whom Halloway needed.

Halloway noticed that Olds had found a second calculator. The two instruments lay side by side on the floor, the fragments of an extended private dialogue flicking to and fro under the Negro's fingers. For the first time Halloway felt impatient.

'Olds—do you want flying lessons or not? If you can't help me I'll find someone else.' Enjoying his aggressive manner, he added, 'Old Buckmaster will know someone.'

I'll help you, Halloway.

For one flying lesson.

So Olds joined Halloway in his grand design. While Halloway drove over to the airport to collect the generators stored in the basement of the car-park, Olds worked away at the apartment block, repairing the elevator and air-conditioning units. With almost magical ease he moved around the building, opening fuse-boxes, trailing cable from a second generator to the motors in the elevator head. When Halloway returned he found Olds serenely raising the elevator like a moody but elegant trapeze artist.

'Olds—its unbelievable ... ' Halloway congratulated him, careful to add, 'Wait until you repair the jet planes at the airport.'

Olds shook his head, watching Halloway reflectively, not taken in by him for a moment.

A little too much – even for me.

'Nothing is – now, we'll help Mr Buckmaster.'

Leaving a dozen stereograms to blare their music into the empty streets, Halloway and Olds set off for the mausoleum. Buckmaster was resting in his bedroom. Flattered by Halloway's concern, he watched with approval from his balcony as Olds manhandled a generator into the lobby and ran the cables up to his suite.

From the breakdown truck Halloway unloaded a battery of six arc-lights he had removed from the façade of the airport terminal building.

'We'll set them up around the square, sir,' Halloway explained. 'At night you'll be able to see the whole monument floodlit.'

Buckmaster strolled across the square, his sharp eyes following Halloway with some curiosity as he darted enthusiastically around the cathedral of cars, setting the arc-lights in position. Deep in the nave of the monument Miranda was at work on the terraces of her hanging garden. Dressed today in blue jeans and a hippy jacket, a child's beads around her wrists, she was placing petunias and nasturtiums among the radiator grilles thirty feet above the ground. During the previous days Halloway had been too busy to make contact with her. Besides, her fey manner unsettled him. There seemed to be something decadent about this obsessive planting of vines and flowers, an unconscious but all the more sinister attempt to bring back a lurid and over-bright nature red in tooth and claw. Halloway had begun to hate the carpets of blossoms, these creepers and climbing plants that threatened to strangle the city before he could release it. Already he was thinking of the defoliants he had noticed in a chemical supplies store.

'I'm grateful to you, Halloway,' Buckmaster told him

as they walked back to the hotel. 'There's a sense of style about you that I like, all too rare these days, you belong to a vanished breed – Brunel, Eiffel, Lloyd Wright, Kaiser, Buckmaster. For once, though, don't pitch your dreams too high. What happens when the gas runs out? You're going to have a second energy crisis all your own.'

Halloway shook his head confidently. 'Sir, there are millions of cars here. The tankers at the airport – some of them are half-full of aviation fuel, enough to keep us going for a year. After that' – Halloway gestured at the air – 'we'll find something else.'

His hand on Halloway's shoulder, Buckmaster listened to the sound of the generator coming to life in the lobby. He watched the arc-lights pulse briefly and then blaze out, almost over-heating the sunshine. For all the old industrialist's caution, Halloway could sense Buckmaster's excitement. Halloway was glad of this. For some reason he wanted to impress him. He was aware that the image of his father, which had propelled him towards the city, had recently begun to fade in his mind, confined to the sailplane tethered like an imprisoned bird on the roof of the car-park.

Halloway pointed at the deserted streets around the square. 'There's so much that should have happened here that never did,' he explained to Buckmaster. 'I want to bring everything alive again, and give back to the city all that lost time.'

During the next weeks Halloway embarked on his grandiose scheme to re-animate the city. From the start he knew that the task of literally bringing back to life the whole of this huge metropolis was beyond the skills of even a hundred men like Olds. However, in a symbolic sense the task could be achieved on a more modest scale.

Adjoining the northern side of the square was a cluster of side-streets that formed a self-sufficient neighbourhood cut off from the fifty-storey buildings surrounding it. By chance, this enclave, little more than a block in extent, contained the whole city in miniature. There were modest hotels and theatres, bars and restaurants, even a police-station and one television studio. Wandering around these narrow streets in the afternoons, Halloway noticed that the stores and offices, banks and supermarkets had been built to a smaller scale than in the rest of the city, and at a time before the zoning ordinances which would have excluded the light factories erected in back-yards, the auto-repair shops in converted garages. On the first floors above the bars and shops were dozens of one-man businesses, minor printing works and travel agencies, tailors and TV repairers.

Sitting on a stool in an empty bar, Halloway calculated that the working population of this city-in-miniature would have been little more than 2000 in its heyday. Even now, a hundred people like himself would be able to get most of its activities going again.

Through the weeks that followed, Halloway and Olds, with grudging help from Stillman, began the task of bringing this neighbourhood back to life. Olds drove in from the airport with a yellow-hulled fuel tanker, filled with enough aviation spirit to power a hundred generators for a month. Tirelessly, he moved in and out of the inspection tunnels below the sidewalks, opening up the electricity sub-stations and feeding down fresh cable. Meanwhile Halloway cut away the tangle of overhead wires that crossed the streets in steel webs, and then he and Olds began the laborious task of re-wiring the roadways. First the street lights came on, filling these deserted thoroughfares with an eerie brilliance, then the traffic signals and pedestrian control signs. Stillman cleared away the hundreds of derelict cars that lined the streets, leaving some twenty vehicles that Olds decided he could renovate.

Supervising all this activity, Halloway drove around in a black-and-white police-car whose engine the young

Negro had brought to life. Halloway had made the local police-station his operational headquarters. The lavish wall-maps and communications equipment, the electric alarm signals that ran to so many of the stores and businesses, even the clandestine listening devices which the police had bugged in to many of the bars and hotels, made the station a natural headquarters.

Often working a dozen hours a day, Halloway pressed on, too tired in the evenings to do more than fall asleep in his apartment two floors below Stillman's. Despite all their efforts, however, the chaos seemed to grow rather than diminish. Piles of garbage covered the sidewalks, dozens of generators and fuel drums blocked the doorways of the bars and supermarkets, everywhere there were sections of dismantled switchboards and circuitry.

But one afternoon, after returning from the airport with a small lathe for Olds, he knew that he had succeeded.

A hundred yards from the station he was approaching a minor street intersection when the traffic lights turned from green to red. Laughing aloud at himself for obeying this solitary signal in an empty city of ten thousand intersections, in which he was its only traffic policeman, Halloway nonetheless pulled to a halt and waited until the lights changed to green. An important principle was at stake. Later, as he sat in the cabin of Stillman's tractor, bulldozing the piles of garbage and collapsed electric signs out of the streets, Halloway reflected that he was not working for himself alone. In the three supermarkets within the reclamation zone he drained the freezer compartments, swept the aisles and re-stacked the pyramids of canned goods, like a dedicated resort hotelier preparing for an invasion army of tourists. Three taxi-cabs, each in running order, stood outside the neighbourhood's leading hotel. One by one the streets were cleared of debris and abandoned cars, the sidewalks were free from garbage, the plate-glass shopfronts gleamed anew.

Amused but impressed by the transformation, Stillman

at last decided to take part. At first, Halloway was reluctant to recruit this deviant figure. Every day Halloway heard him moving around the city, the violent explosions of breaking steel and glass as he dragged down another department-store portico and ran his tracks over the mannequins. In the evenings, as they sat together on the flood-lit terrace of the penthouse, Stillman would gaze resentfully across the roasting deer, as if annoyed that the dark dream of the city which had sustained him for so long should be brought to life in so naive a fashion by this idealistic youth. Then, one evening when Halloway was rhapsodizing about the harshness and vitality of his neat and immaculate streets, Stillman brusquely shut him up and announced that he would join the reclamation project. Clearly he had decided to inject some real life into this toy-town neighbourhood. He curtly turned down Halloway's suggestion that he take over the renovation of a store selling kitchen equipment.

'That's not my style, Halloway. I leave the domestic sciences to you. My expertise lies in other areas ... '

In no time Stillman had staked out two amusement arcades, several bars and a small nightclub in the basement of an office block. Once Olds had supplied electric current Stillman set to work with a will, moving at a far swifter pace than his usual surly languor had ever previously allowed. The amusement arcades were soon a blaze of garish lights. Pinball machines chattered and clanged, score numerals stuttered. In the communications room of the police-station Halloway sat by the monitor screen of the traffic-control television system, watching the multicoloured lights ripple across the sidewalks.

Stillman had stripped down the punctured neon signs above the bars and arcades. From a warehouse discovered somewhere he brought in a truckload of intact signs, massive pieces of electrographic architecture that dominated the whole of Halloway's neighbourhood. Giant letters dripped across the night sky, cascades of pink light fell mushily across the façade of his nightclub, the winged emblems of long-vanished airlines pulsed through the overloaded air, the roof-sills of bars and amusement arcades were trimmed with tubes of racing fluorescence.

Watching uneasily on his TV monitor, Halloway wondered how to put a stop to this lurid invasion. At dusk, as the surrounding city grew dark, he left the police-station and cruised the streets in his squad-car, listening to the generators beating in the basements and alleyways, the tireless hearts pumping out this haemorrhage of light. He knew now why Stillman had been so dismissive of his laborious restocking of offices and supermarkets. It was only now, in this raucous light and noise, that the city was being its true self, only in this flood of cheap neon that it was really alive.

Halloway parked outside a bank he had begun to reclaim. Olds' tool-bags and equipment trolleys were by the doorway. He had been working on the electrically-operated vault doors before leaving for the airport, and the piles of old banknotes lay exposed in their metal trays. Halloway looked down at the bales of notes, worthless now but a fortune thirty years earlier. In Garden City money was never used, and had given way to a sophisticated system of barter and tithes-giving that eliminated the abuses of credit, instalment-buying and taxation.

Touching the banknotes, with their subtle progression from one denomination to the next, a means of quantifying the value of everything, its promise and obligation, Halloway watched the garish lights of the neon signs in the street flicker across his hands. He was glad that Stillman had transformed this staid and well-swept thoroughfare. They needed workers for the stores and offices and production lines, and they needed visitors for the hotels and bars. They would need money, as well, to oil the engine of competition.

Halloway locked away the trays of banknotes and

slipped the keys into his pocket. There were thousands of other banks in the city, but in the printing shop next to the police station Olds would over-print the notes with Halloway's frank. The thought pleased him – to have reached the point of issuing his own currency meant that success was really at hand.

He ended his evening rounds at the square. Lit by the arc-lights, Buckmaster's memorial of cars rose over three hundred feet into the air, a cathedral of rust. The vines and flowers that climbed its sides looked dead in the fierce light. Halloway was glad to see that their once vivid colours were blanched out by the powerful glare. A dozen reflections in the dark buildings around the square transformed it into a mortuary plain of illuminated tombs.

Buckmaster stood on the steps of his hotel, looking with obvious pleasure at this huge spectacle. Miranda, however, watching from a window above, stared at Halloway with equally clear hostility. That afternoon Halloway had stripped the last of the poppies and forget-me-nots from the avenues around the reclamation zone. As he crossed the square at the controls of the tractor, the bale of flowers in the metal scoop like a multicoloured haystack, Miranda followed him through the streets, catching in her white hands the loose petals that drifted in the air.

Now, on her balcony, she was dressed in a bizarre Barbarella costume of silver metal and glass, like a science-fiction witch about to take her revenge on Halloway.

Unaware of his daughter's anger, Buckmaster took Halloway's arm and pointed to a building across the square, the offices of a former newspaper. A frieze of electric letters that had once carried a continuous news strip had been repaired by Olds, a city-sized replica of the display panels of his pocket calculators. Letters began to race from right to left.

'Halloway, they ought to hand you the mayoral chain,

my boy, and put your name up there, high, wide and handsome!'

But already the first message was flashing past.

OLDS! OLDS! OLDS! OLDS! OLDS!

Delighted by this, Halloway joined Buckmaster and rode the elevator with the old industrialist to the observation platform beside his cathedral. As they stepped out, however, a new message was racing across the display sign.

DANGER! FIVE MILES NORTH-EAST. INVASION PARTY COMING.

Two days later, when the rescue expedition arrived, Halloway was ready to deal with them in his own way. During that first night after Olds had given the alarm he spent the long hours until dawn in the top-floor offices of the newspaper building. Soon after sunrise he watched the landing party disembark from their sailing vessel, a three-master whose white aluminium sails and white steel hull stood out against the dark water like chiselled bone. Using binoculars, Halloway immediately identified the ship, a barquentine built by the Garden City administrative council.

Halloway had taken for granted that a rescue party would one day come to search for him. Presumably they had been scouring the shore along the northern coast of the Sound, and had now decided to explore the city itself, no doubt guided there by the sudden efflorescence of light each evening, this neon pleasure-drome that had come to life among the silent tower-blocks.

An hour after dawn Halloway drove north through the city in his squad-car. He left the vehicle half a mile from the landing point and walked ahead through the deserted streets. The white masts and square metal fore-sail of the barquentine rose above the buildings near the quay where she had docked. There was no rigging—remote-controlled by an in-board computer that assessed tides, course and wind-velocity, the ship was the ultimate in the technology of sail.

Halloway climbed on to the roof of an appliance store and watched the expedition party come ashore. There were ten people in the group, all members of the Garden City gliding club – Halloway recognized the architect and his twelve-year-old son, and the elderly hydrographer with the red beard. As they unloaded their bicycles and wicker hampers they reminded Halloway of a Victorian picnic party exploring a nature reserve. Had he really spent his life with these quiet, civilized and anaemic people? Amused by them, but already bored by the whole absurd business, he watched them adjust their bicycle clips and tyre pressures. Their polite and gentle manners, the timid way in which they gazed down the empty streets, had given him all the ideas he needed on how to deal with them.

As Halloway had guessed, it took the rescue party a full two days to reach the centre of the city. During the mornings they pedalled forward at a sedate pace, cautiously making their way through the abandoned cars and festoons of rusting telephone wire. There were endless pauses to consult their maps and take refreshment. They had even brought a portable recycling unit with them, and carefully reprocessed their kitchen and other wastes. By early afternoon they were already pitching their elaborate tents and laying out their complex camping equipment.

Luckily, it was almost dusk when they finally reached the central square. On the television monitor in the police-station Halloway watched them dismount from their bicycles and stare with amazement at Buckmaster's towering monument. Lit by a single floodlight inside the nave the memorial rose above the darkened square, the hundreds of windows and radiator grilles shining like the facets of an immense glowing jewel.

The party edged forward tentatively, gripping their bicycle handlebars for moral support. All around them the streets were dark and silent. Then, as they all bent down to take off their trouser clips, Halloway leaned across his control console and began to throw the switches.

Later, when he looked back on this episode, Halloway relished his routing of the rescue party and only wished that he had recorded it on the traffic control video-tape system. For thirty minutes total pandemonium had broken loose in the square and nearby streets. As a hundred generators roared into life, pouring electric current into the grid, arc-lights blazed around the square, freezing his would-be rescuers in their tracks. The façades of the buildings around the square erupted into a cataract of neon. Traffic lights beckoned and signalled. From the loudspeakers which Olds had strung across the streets came a babel of sound – police sirens howling, jet aircraft taking off, trains slamming through junctions, car horns blaring, all the noises of the city in its heyday which Halloway had found in a speciality record shop.

As this visual and acoustic nightmare broke loose around the members of the rescue party, Halloway left the communications room and ran down to the street. As he climbed into his police-car Stillman swerved past in his white gangster's limousine. Racing after him, Halloway switched on his siren. He reached the square and hurtled around it, cornering on two wheels in the way approved by the stunt-drivers in the fifty-year-old crime films which Stillman had screened for him in his nightclub that afternoon.

For the next fifteen minutes, as the noise of police sirens and aircraft, machine-gun fire and express trains sounded through the streets, Halloway and Stillman put on their mock car chase, pursuing each other around the square, plunging out of narrow alleys and swerving across the sidewalks, driving the terrified members of the rescue party in front of them. Stillman, inevitably, soon went too far, knocking the bicycles out of their hands and crushing two of the complex machines against a fire hydrant. In fact, Halloway was certain that if they had not turned tail and run at least one member of the party would have been killed.

Abandoning their equipment and sharing the remaining bicycles, it took them less than six hours to reach the ship and set sail. Long after they had gone, when Halloway had switched off the recorded sounds and dimmed the neon lights, Stillman continued to drive around the square in his white limousine, jumping the lights at the traffic intersections, tirelessly wheeling the big car in and out of the alleys and side-streets, as if deranged by this dream-come-true of the violent city.

From the communications room at the police-station Halloway watched Stillman's car swerving around the square. Somehow he would have to find a means of containing Stillman before he destroyed everything they had done. Tired out by all the noise and action, Halloway reached forward to switch off the monitor, when he realized that he was no longer the only spectator of Stillman's disturbed driving.

Standing in the portico of a deserted bank, their slim figures almost hidden by the high columns, were two boys in their late teens. Despite the shiny plastic suitcases and their flamboyant shoes and jackets—presumably taken from the stores on the outskirts of the city—Halloway was certain that they had come from one of the pastoral settlements. On their Garden City faces was a childlike expectation, an innocent but clear determination to seize the life of the metropolis.

Switching on the loudspeaker system so that he could talk to them, Halloway picked up the microphone. The first of his people had arrived to take their places in his city.

* * *

It had been another successful day. On the television monitor in the police commissioner's office Halloway watched the activity in the avenue below. It was five o'clock in the afternoon, and the rush-hour traffic was beginning to build up. The sidewalks were thronged by more than a dozen pedestrians, leaving their offices and workshops on their way to the neighbourhood bars and supermarkets. A hundred yards from the station, six cars were blocking an intersection where the lights had failed. Their horns sounded impatiently above the street noise.

Halloway spoke to the desk sergeant in the orderly room. 'Get a man over to the Seventh Avenue intersection. There's a faulty green light holding up the traffic.'

'He's already left, Mr Halloway.'

'Good – if we don't watch it now there'll be chaos in an hour or two.'

These minor breakdowns were a pleasant challenge to Halloway. Even now, as one of Stillman's young men ignored the stuttering red light and the outstretched arm of the police constable, Halloway was in no way annoyed. In a sense, these displays of aggression pleased him, confirming everything he had hoped about the reclamation scheme. The pedestrians in the street below strode along purposefully, pushing past each other with scant courtesy. There was no trace here of good humour and pastoral docility.

In an alleyway facing the station a diesel generator was pumping out dense clouds of sooty smoke. A three-man repair gang recently trained by Olds had emptied the sump oil across the sidewalk, in clear contravention of the local ordinances. But, again, Halloway made no attempt to reprimand them. If anything, he had done what he could to frustrate any efforts to bring in stricter clear-air regulations. Pollution was part of the city, a measure of its health. All the so-called ills that had beset this huge metropolis in its prime had visited themselves with flattering haste on Halloway's small enclave. Pollution, traffic congestion, inadequate municipal services, inflation and deficit public financing had all promptly re-appeared.

Halloway had even been pleased when the first crime was committed. During the previous night several clothing stores had been broken into, and pilfering from the supermarkets went on continuously. Halloway had spoken to Stillman about the light-fingered behaviour of his entourage. Lounging back with his young cronies in his 1920s gangster limousine, Stillman had merely flicked the sharp lapels of his dove-grey suit and pointed out that petty crime helped to keep the economy running.

'Relax, Halloway, it's all part of the problem of urban renewal. Do I complain that some of your boys are on the take? You've got to increase turnover. You're working these poor devils so hard they haven't time to spend their pay. If they've got anything left by the end of the week, that is. This is a real high-rent area you've set up for them. Any time now you'll have a housing crisis on your hands, social problems, urban unrest. Remember, Halloway, you don't want to start a flight from the cities.'

Halloway had taken this friendly ribbing in his stride, though the rapid increase in the size of Stillman's gang had begun to make him uneasy. Clearly Stillman relished lording it over this entourage of wide-eyed teenagers and farm-bred youths, fitting them up with their gangster suits and weapons like a corrupt stage-director playing ironic games with a chorus of young actors. At times Halloway felt that he too was part of this sardonic man's devious entertainment.

However, apart from the stealing, Stillman's continued ravaging of department store windows in the surrounding districts of the city had turned Halloway's neighbourhood into an island of light and activity in an ever-larger sea of devastation. Halloway's plans for expansion had been effectively shelved by this deliberate vandalism, the wholesale destruction of complete city blocks.

In addition, Stillman's entourage had come into collision with Olds, and Halloway now depended more than ever on the mute. Two of Stillman's men had tried to break into Olds' automobile plant, complaining that the models they had ordered from him had not been delivered. For several days Olds had retreated to his rooftop eyrie above the garage at the airport. Without him everything soon began to run down. Halloway drove out to pacify him, and found Olds sitting below the wing of the glider tethered to the roof, calculators flicking in his hands as he brooded to himself. His eyes were gazing at the flights of birds taking off from the reservoirs around the airport, thousands of wild geese moving westwards across the city. Uneasily, Halloway noticed that the cars in his museum were still dusty and untended. One of them, the black Duesenberg, had been savagely attacked, its windows knocked in and upholstery slashed, controls pounded out of recognition by a heavy mallet.

But for a brilliant stroke of Halloway's, Olds would long since have left. Two months beforehand, he had shown his first irritation with the throngs of youths and teenage girls who were entering the reclamation area. Many of them were idealists like Halloway, repressed by the passivity of the garden communities and eager to help re-start the city. However, an equal number were drifters and misfits, who resented taking orders from Olds and began to mimic him, flashing obscenities on the read-out panels of the pocket calculators they had taken from a business-machines store.

Searching for some way of retaining his hold over Olds, Halloway came up with the suggestion that the mute could own and manage his own automobile plant. The idea had immediately appealed to Olds. In an underground garage near the police-station he and his work-force soon constructed a crude but functioning production line, on which the dozens of cars being re-equipped and re-engined moved along a section of railway line. They entered as little more than wrecks picked up off the street by their prospective owners, and emerged at the far end of the line as fully functioning vehicles. Delighted by this, Olds had agreed to stay on in the city.

In fact, Halloway's idea worked better than he hoped. The motor-car was the chief commodity of the city, and demand for it was insatiable. Almost every one of the new inhabitants now owned three or four cars, and their chief recreation was driving around the streets of the reclamation area dressed in the latest finery. Parking problems had become acute, and a special task force under Olds was renovating the kerbside meters, an unpopular measure grudgingly accepted only because of the special status of the automobile and the important position it occupied, economically and otherwise, in people's lives.

Despite these problems, Halloway was satisfied with his achievement. In the four months since the first of the new arrivals had turned up, a genuine microcosm of the former metropolis had come into existence. The population of the city was now two hundred, girls and youths in their late teens and early twenties, emigrants from Garden City and Parkville, Laurel Heights and Heliopolis, drawn from these dozy pastoral settlements to the harsh neon glare that each evening lit up the night sky like a beacon.

By now any new immigrants – some of them, worryingly, little more than children – were rapidly inducted into urban life. On arrival they were interviewed by Halloway, issued with a list of possible jobs, either on Olds' production line, in the clothing stores and supermarkets, or in any one of a dozen reclamation gangs. The last group, who foraged through the city at large for cars, fuel, food supplies, tools and electrical equipment, in effect represented the productive capacity of the new settlement, but in time Halloway hoped that they would embark on the original manufacture of an ever-wider range of consumer goods. Cash credits (banknotes franked with Halloway's name) were advanced to the new recruits against their first week's pay, with which they could buy the garish clothing, records and cigarettes they seemed to need above all else. Most of the two hundred inhabitants were now heavily in debt, but rather than evict them from their apartments and close the discotheques, bars and amusement arcades where they spent their evenings, Halloway had astutely lengthened the working day from eight to ten hours, enticing them with generous though uneconomic overtime payments. Already, he happily realized, he was literally printing money. Within only a few months inflation would be rampant, but like the crime and pollution this was a real sign of his success, a confirmation of all he had dreamed about.

There was a flicker of interference on the monitor screen, indicating a fault in the camera mounted outside the station. Muttering with mock-annoyance, 'Nothing works any more,' Halloway switched to the camera in the square. The open plaza with its memorial of cars was deserted at this hour. The monument had never been completed. Stillman had long since lost interest in the hard work of construction, and no one else had volunteered, particularly as no payment was involved. Besides, these memorials of cars and radiator grilles, tyres and kitchen appliances created an atmosphere of defeat and fatality, presiding like funeral pyres over the outskirts of the city as the new arrivals pressed on to their promised land.

A few attempts had been made to dismantle the pyramids, but each time Buckmaster and his daughter had managed to make good the damage. Dressed in her ever-changing costumes, in this cavalcade of Twentieth-Century fashion, Miranda moved tirelessly through the city, seeding the glass-filled streets with poppies and daisies, trailing vines over the fallen telephone wires. Halloway had given two assistants the task of following her around the city and destroying whatever new plants they could find. Too many of the flowers she was now setting out in window boxes and ornamental urns had a distinctly sinister aspect. Halloway had caught her the previous week, eerily at work in the reclamation area itself, bedding out bizarre lilies with nacreous petals and mantis-like flowers in the entrance to the police-station, glamorous but vicious plants that looked as if they might lunge at the throats of anyone passing by. Halloway had pushed past her, overturned her flower trolley and torn out the lilies with his bare hands. Then, with unexpected forbearance, he had ordered his sergeant to drive her back to her hotel. His feelings for Miranda remained as confused as they had been at their first meeting. On the one hand he wanted to impress her, to make her recognize the importance of everything he had done, on the other he was vaguely afraid of this young and naive Diana of the botanical gardens, about to embark on some macabre hunt through the intense, over-heated foliage.

The day after this incident Buckmaster paid Halloway a visit, the first he had made to the reclamation zone. Still keen to earn the old industrialist's approval, Halloway took him on a tour of the neighbourhood, proudly pointing out the mechanics working on the motor-cars on Olds' production line, the gleaming vehicles being collected by their new owners, the system of credit and finance which he had evolved, the busy bars and supermarkets, the new arrivals moving into their refurbished apartments, and even the first two-hour-a-day transmissions from the local television station – the programmes, with complete historical accuracy, consisted entirely of old movies and commercials. The latter, despite a hiatus of thirty years, were still up-to-date advertisements of the products they bought and sold in the stores and supermarkets.

'Everything is here that you can think of, sir,' Halloway

told the old man. 'And it's a living urban structure, not a film set. We've got traffic problems, inflation, even the beginnings of serious crime and pollution ...'

The industrialist smiled at Halloway in a not unkindly way. 'That's a proud boast, Halloway. I'd begun to notice those last two myself. Now, you've taken me on your tour – let me take you on one of mine.'

Reluctant to leave his command post in the commissioner's office, Halloway nonetheless decided to humour Buckmaster. Besides, he knew that in many ways Buckmaster had taken over the role of his own father. Often, as he relaxed in the evenings at his apartment overlooking the park, Halloway seriously wondered if his father would have understood all that he had achieved, so far beyond the antique engine parts and aircraft designs. Unhappily, Buckmaster – who certainly did understand – remained ambiguous in his response.

Together they set off in Halloway's car, driving for over an hour towards the industrial areas to the north-west of the city. Here, among the power stations and railyards, foundries and coal depots, Buckmaster tried to point out to Halloway how the Twentieth Century had met its self-made death. They stood on the shores of artificial lagoons filled with chemical wastes, drove along canals silvered by metallic scum, across landscapes covered by thousands of tons of untreated garbage, fields piled high with cans, broken glass and derelict machinery.

But as he listened to the old man warning him that sooner or later he would add to these terminal moraines, Halloway had been exhilarated by the scenes around him. Far from disfiguring the landscape, these discarded products of Twentieth-Century industry had a fierce and wayward beauty. Halloway was fascinated by the glimmering sheen of the metal-scummed canals, by the strange submarine melancholy of drowned cars looming up at him from abandoned lakes, by the brilliant colours of the garbage hills, by the glitter of a million cans embedded in a matrix of detergent packs and tinfoil, a kaleidoscope of everything they could wear, eat and drink. He was fascinated by the cobalt clouds that drifted below the surface of the water, free at last of all plants and fish, the soft chemical billows interacting as they seeped from the sodden soil. He explored the whorls of steel shavings, foliage culled from a metallic christmas tree, the bales of rusting wire whose dense copper hues formed a burnished forest in the sunlight. He gazed raptly at the chalky whiteness of old china-clay tips, vivid as powdered ice, abandoned railyards with their moss-covered locomotives, the undimmed beauty of industrial wastes produced by skills and imaginations far richer than nature's, more splendid than any Arcadian meadow. Unlike nature, here there was no death.

Lulled by this vision of technology's Elysian Fields, Halloway sat half-asleep behind the commissioner's desk, dwarfed by the leather-backed chair. When he woke he found that the TV monitor was again showing a jumble of interference patterns. Part of the excitement of city life was the constant breakdown of these poorly designed appliances, and the difficulty of getting hold of a repairman. In Garden City, every piece of equipment, every washing machine and solar-powered kitchen stove, functioned forever with dismaying perfection. In the rare event of even the smallest malfunction the designer would appear on one's doorstep as fast as his bicycle could carry him. By contrast, the metropolis operated an exciting knife-edge away from total collapse.

Leaving the station, Halloway saluted the two eighteen-year-old policemen sitting in their patrol car. There were ten officers under his command, an over-large proportion of the total number of inhabitants, but all Halloway's scrutiny of the commissioner's records confirmed that a large police-force, like pollution and a high crime-rate, was an essential feature of city life.

Besides, they might well be useful sooner than he expected. As he stepped into his car to drive the fifty yards to Olds' garage – Halloway never walked, however short the distance, and often U-turned his car to get from one side of the road to the other – a gang of teenage boys tumbled with a chorus of obscenities from a nearby amusement arcade. They clustered around a large motorcycle with extended forks and a lavishly chromed engine. All wore black leather jackets strung with sinister ornaments – iron crosses, ceremonial daggers and death's heads. The driver kick-started the machine with a violent roar, then lurched in a circle across the sidewalk, knocking down part of a tobacco kiosk before veering into Halloway's path. Without apology, he drummed his fist on the roof above Halloway's head and roared off down the street, weaving in and out of the shouting pedestrians.

As Halloway expected, most of the workers on Olds' production line had packed up early. The thirty vehicles mounted on their movable trolleys had come to a halt, and the few mechanics left were plugging the batteries into the overnight chargers.

Olds was seated in his glass-walled office, moodily playing with his collection of pocket calculators, slim fingers flicking out fragments of some strange dialogue. As life for him had become increasingly complex, with all the problems of running this automobile plant, he had added more and more calculators. He placed the instruments in a series of lines across his desk, and seemed to be working towards a decision about everything, laying out the elements of this reductive conversation like cards in a game of solitaire.

He gazed up at Halloway, as if recognizing him with difficulty. He looked tired and listless, numbed by his work on all the projects which Halloway pushed forward ruthlessly.

'Olds, it's only six. Why are we scrapping the evening shift?'

There are not enough men for the line.

'They should all be here.' When Olds sat back, shuffling the calculators with one hand, Halloway snapped, 'Olds – they need the work! They've got to pay back their wage credits!'

The mute shrugged, watching Halloway with his passive but intelligent eyes. From a drawer he pulled out his old flying-helmet. He seemed about to question Halloway about something, but changed his mind.

Halloway, they lack your appreciation of the value of hard work.

'Olds, can't you understand?' With an effort, Halloway controlled his exasperation. He paced around the office, deciding on a new tack. 'Listen, Olds, there's something I wanted to bring up with you. As you know, you don't actually pay any rent for this garage – in fact, this whole operation makes no direct contribution at all to the municipal budget. Originally I exempted you because of the help you've given in starting everything up, but I think now we'll have to look into the question of some kind of reasonable rent – and of taxation, too, for that matter.' As Olds' fingers began to race irritatingly across the calculators, flicking out a series of messages he was unable to read, Halloway pressed on.

'There's another thing. So much of life here depends on time – hours of work, rates of pay and so on, they're all hitched to the clock. It occurred to me that if we lengthened the hour, without anyone knowing, of course, we would get more work out of people for the same rates of pay. Suppose I ordered in all the clocks and wristwatches, for a free check-up, say, could you readjust them so that they ran a little slower?' Halloway paused, waiting to see if Olds fully appreciated the simplicity of this ingenious scheme. He added, 'Naturally, it would be to everyone's benefit. In fact, by varying the length of the hour, by slowing or speeding up all the clocks, we would have a powerful economic regulator, we'd be able to cut back or encourage inflation, vary pay-rates and productivity. I'm looking ahead, I know, but I already visualize a central radio transmitter beaming out a variable time signal to everyone's clock and wristwatch, so that no one need bother about making the adjustments himself ...'

Halloway waited for a reply, but the calculators were silent for once, their display panels unlit. Olds was looking up at him with an expression Halloway had never seen before. All the mute's intelligence and judgment were in his eyes, staring at this blond-haired young man as if seeing him clearly for the first time.

Annoyed by his almost disdainful attitude, Halloway was tempted to strike the mute. But at that moment, carried clearly above the drumming of the generators, they heard the squeal of tyres in the road above, and the sounds of breaking glass and a child's scream.

When they reached the street a crowd had already gathered, standing around a white limousine that had swerved across the sidewalk and plunged through the windows of a supermarket. Cans and detergent packs, which Halloway had helped to stack into their display pyramids, were scattered among the broken glass. Stillman's chauffeur, a black-jacketed youth of sixteen, stepped from the car, spitting away his gum in a nervous gesture. Everyone was looking down at two eleven-year-old boys, barely conscious, stretched out in the roadway, and at the dead body of a young girl lying under the limousine between its rear wheels.

As the siren of a police-car wailed towards them Olds pushed through the crowd. He knelt down and held the girl's bloodied wrist. When he carried her away in his arms, pushing brusquely past Halloway, he held the calculator in one hand. Halloway caught a glimpse of its display panel, screaming out a single silent obscenity.

The next week marked an uneasy interregnum. On the pretext of keeping an eye on everything, Halloway retreated to the commissioner's office, watching the streets for hours on the TV monitor. The death of the girl, the first traffic fatality of the new city, was an event even Halloway was unable to rationalize. He stayed away from the funeral, which was attended by everyone except himself. Olds drove the huge hearse, which he found in a breaker's yard and spent all night refurbishing. Surrounded by an arbour of flowers, the dead child in her lavish hand-carved casket moved away at the head of the procession, followed through the empty streets by all the people of the neighbourhood, everyone at the wheel of his car. Stillman and his entourage wore their darkest gangster suits. Miranda and old Buckmaster, both in black capes, appeared in an ancient open tourer filled with strange wreaths she had prepared from the flowers that Halloway's men had destroyed.

However, much to Halloway's relief everything soon returned to normal, though by some unhappy paradox this first death set off an even greater latent violence. During the following days more and more workers defected from their jobs to join Stillman's entourage, which by now had swollen to a substantial private army. Many of them wore black para-military uniforms. All day the sound of gunfire echoed through the streets as they destroyed hundreds of the deer in the park, driving away the pheasants, quail and wild duck on which Halloway depended to stock the fresh meat counters of the supermarkets. Armed with rifles, they marched up and down the square in parade order, presenting arms beside the files of slaughtered deer. Stillman, now affecting a military tunic and peaked cap, had swapped his limousine for an open-topped half-track, in which he stood to attention, taking the salute.

Halloway tried to laugh off these absurd games as another mental aberration of this convicted murderer, but Stillman's men had begun to disrupt the life of the zone. They strolled in gangs around the supermarkets, helping themselves to whatever they wanted and brushing aside any requests for payment. Taking their cue from this, many of the apartment-house tenants defaulted on their rents. Instead of shopping at the supermarkets, and helping to bolster the faltering economy of the zone, they were breaking into the stores outside the area. Each day there was a further slide towards anarchy, the failure of another generator, an increase in traffic delays and parking offences, and above all a growing conviction that the city was unmanageable.

Faced with this collapse of his dream, worked for with such effort, Halloway decided to reassert his authority. He needed some means of inspiring these new urban dwellers. Bored by their long hours of repetitive work, most of them did no more in their leisure time than hang around the bars and amusement arcades, driving aimlessly around the streets in their various cars. The influx of new arrivals had begun to fall off, and already the first of the original settlers were packing their bags and drifting off to the suburbs.

After a night of continuous uproar, filled with the sound of sirens and gunfire, Halloway decided to enlist Buckmaster's help. The old industrialist was the only person he could fall back on. Olds no longer spoke to him – the whole make-believe of teaching the mute to fly had long since lost its credibility. But Buckmaster had been one of the pioneers who created the Twentieth Century, and might well be able to charge everyone with enthusiasm again.

Outside Buckmaster's hotel Halloway hesitated before stepping from his car. His ruthless use of defoliants on Miranda's plant kingdom made him uneasy about seeing her, but he would have to brush this aside.

As he climbed the steps to the hotel entrance he noticed that the revolving door had been converted into a miniature greenhouse. Each of the segments was filled with an unfamiliar plant, with purple flowers and purple-black berries. With a reflex of irritation, Halloway was about to rip them out with his hands, but a brief movement on a balcony above him caught his eye.

Three floors above, Miranda was standing on her balcony and looking down at Halloway, a posy of mantis lilies in her hand. She was wearing a long white dress and white lace veil that Halloway had never seen before, but which he recognized immediately. Gazing up at her, and knowing that she had never been more beautiful, Halloway was suddenly convinced that she was wearing the wedding gown for him. She was waiting for Halloway to come and collect her from the hotel, and then they would cross the square to the cathedral of cars where her father would marry them.

As if to confirm this, Miranda leaned slightly over her balcony, smiling at Halloway and beckoning to him with a white-gloved hand.

When he reached the revolving door the purple flowers and dark berries clustered thickly around him. He was about to push past them when he remembered the posy of lilies in her hand, and the too-eager way in which she had watched him arrive. Then he realized that the plants he was about to brush out of his way, festering here in this glass execution chamber between himself and his bride, were deadly nightshade.

In the early afternoon Miranda and her father left the city for good.

That night, as he lay asleep in his apartment, Halloway dreamed that he was standing at an open window overlooking the park. Below him the waist-high grass shivered and seethed. Some deep motion had unsettled the ground, a profound shudder that crossed the entire park. The bushes and brambles, the trees and shrubs, even the lowliest weeds and wild flowers, were beginning to rustle and quiver, straining from the ground. Everywhere branches were waving in an invisible wind, leaves beating at the passing air. Then, by the lake at the centre of the park, a miniature oak broke free, boughs moving like the wings of an ungainly bird. Shaking the earth from its roots, it soared towards Halloway, a hundred feet from the ground. Other trees were following, branches grasping at the air, a million leaves whirling together. As Halloway watched, gripping the window-sill to stop himself from joining them, the whole park suddenly rose upwards, every tree and flower, every blade of grass joining to form an immense sunlit armada that circled above Halloway's head and soared along the rays of the sun. As they moved away across the sky Halloway could see that all over the city the flowers and vines which Miranda had planted were also leaving. A flight of poppies soared past, a crimson carpet followed by an aerial causeway of daisies, petals beating as if they were the cilia of some huge lace-like creature. Halloway looked up from the city, with its now barren stone and dying air. The sky was filled with a legion of flying creatures, a green haze of petals and blossoms free at last to make their way to the welcoming sun.

When he woke the next morning, Halloway went out on to his balcony, uncertain whether the dense vegetation rooted securely to the ground was an illusion of his mind. Later, when he paused briefly at the police-station, the vision of these flying oaks and marigolds, elms and daisies still hung in the air, brighter than the neon façades of the bars and amusement arcades.

Instead of switching off the lights and going to work, people were hanging around the doorways of the bars, watching Halloway across the pin-tables in the arcades. None of the police-force had turned up for duty, and for a moment Halloway felt that the day itself had failed to appear.

Determined now on a confrontation with Stillman, he

went back to his car. He was convinced that the former convict was responsible for the collapse of everything he had worked for. Stillman had been drawn here by the limitless opportunities he had seen for cruelty and disruption. He needed a dying city, not a living one, a warm cadaver that he could infest like a maggot.

After locking the police-station, Halloway drove along the park to Stillman's headquarters, a cylindrical art museum with a single spiral ramp that circled upwards to Stillman's audience chamber. Armed guards lounged in their black uniforms around the line of armoured limousines parked outside. They signalled Halloway forward, clearly expecting him. As Halloway walked towards the elevator Stillman was standing in a theatrical pose on the topmost stage.

Their meeting never took place. Half way up, the elevator stopped with an abrupt shudder, its lights failing. Everywhere voices began to shout, a shot was fired, feet raced past down the ramp. By the time Halloway broke free from the elevator he was the last to leave the darkened building. Stillman and his gang had set off, taking Halloway's car with them.

When he reached the police-station half an hour later an electrical storm was sweeping the streets of the reclamation zone. Cars were stalled bumper to bumper at the intersections. The drivers stood by their vehicles, flinching from the neon signs that were exploding in cascades of molten glass above the bars and restaurants. Everywhere the overloaded circuitry was burning out. Coloured light-bulbs burst and ripped across the ceilings of the amusement arcades. Pin-tables exploded in a chatter of free games, in the supermarkets the first fires were lifting from the freezer cabinets, flames roasting the carcasses of the deer and wild-fowl. The noise of a hundred generators filled the air, turned up by someone to their greatest output.

It took Halloway several hours to restore order. Long

before he had turned down the last of the overheated generators, replaced the fuses and put out the most serious of the fires, Halloway knew who had been responsible. Dozens of the pocket calculators lay around the generators in the alleyways and basements, display panels glowing dimly. Olds must have ransacked the business-machine stores, gathering together as many calculators as he could find to cope with his mental crisis. They were scattered in his trail, spinning off from his hyper-active mind.

Wings?

Mixture rich, carburettor heat cold.

Sparrow, wren, robin, hummingbird ...

Halloway stared down angrily at these fragmentary messages, bulletins to himself that expressed Olds' doubts and anxieties. When Halloway found him he would scream him into submission with one potent word, throw him into a final fit from which he would never recover.

Kiwi, penguin?

Pitch full fine, fuel cocks open.

Starling, swallow, swift ...

Halloway stamped on the calculators, pulverizing this ascending order of birds. Exhausted by the effort of shutting down the generators, he sat on the floor in the supermarket basement, surrounded by soup cans and the glowing dials.

Climbing.

Flaps down, throttle slightly cracked.

Elizabeth, dead child. No pain.

Blue eyes. Insane.

Partridge, quail, geese, oriole ... eagle, osprey, falcon ...

Guessing that he might find the mute in his automobile plant, Halloway ran down the ramp into the basement. But Olds had gone. In a last galvanic spasm, the thirty cars on the production line had been hurled against the concrete wall, and lay heaped across each other in a tangle of chrome and broken glass. On the desk in his office the calculators were laid out neatly to form a last message.

Ol

Old

Olds

Oldsm

Oldsmo

Oldsmob

Oldsmobi

Oldsmobil

OLDSMOBILE!!!

And then, in the drawer where he had kept his antique flying-helmet:

I can—!

Fulmar, albatross, flamingo, frigate-bird, condor ...

IGNITION!

Abandoning his car, Halloway walked through the empty streets, littered with smouldering neon tubes as if a burnt-out rainbow had collapsed across the sidewalks. Already he could see that everyone had gathered in the square, their backs turned to Buckmaster's memorial. They were looking up at the display sign on the newspaper building, the brief message which Olds had left for them repeating itself in a cry of fear, pride and determination.

I CAN FLY! I CAN FLY! I CAN FLY! I CAN FLY!

By the time Halloway reached the airport the siege was well under way. Stillman and his men surrounded the car-park, crouching behind their limousines and firing at random at the upper floors. There were no signs of Olds, but from the apex of the pyramid of radiator grilles Halloway could see that the powered glider on the roof had been readied for flight. Olds had fitted an undercarriage and tail-wheel to the craft. No longer tethered, it had been moved to the upper end of the canted roof, the two hundred yards of concrete sloping away below the polished propeller.

Under cover of a fusillade of shots, Stillman and three of his men rushed the building and entered the ground floor of the car-park. Ten storeys above them, Olds appeared on the roof, dressed in his antique flying-suit, leather jacket and gaiters. He moved around the aircraft, making some last adjustments to the engine, oblivious of the shooting below.

Twenty minutes later, smoke began to rise from the eighth floor of the car-park, dark billows that lifted towards the roof. Seeing the smoke, Olds stopped and watched it swirl around him. Then, above the sound of gunshots and exploding fuel tanks, Halloway heard the clatter of the aero-engine. The propeller span briskly, pumping the heavy smoke out of its way.

Knowing that Olds would be killed if he tried to take off, Halloway ran towards the car-park. Shouting at Stillman's men, he pushed past them to the emergency stairs.

When he reached the eighth floor one of the young guards held him back. At the far end of the sloping concrete floor Olds had built a solid barricade with his four land-cruisers. Unable to climb past it, and with the remainder of the stairway blocked by a pile of generators and electrical equipment, Stillman and his men were setting fire to the cars, shooting into the engine compartments and fuel tanks of these once-cherished sedans and limousines.

'Stillman!' Halloway shouted. 'Let him go! If he tries to fly he'll kill himself!'

But Stillman waved him away. Two of the cars were burning briskly, and he and his men pushed the flaming vehicles up the slope and rammed them into the land-cruisers. Within moments the metal cabins were splitting in the fierce heat. Watching this conflagration begin, Stillman beckoned his men down the slope.

Then, moving down the gutter below the internal balustrade, came a thin stream of fluid, working its way around the old tyres and the piles of leaves and birds' nests. Thinking that this was Olds' pathetic attempt to douse the fire Stillman had started, Halloway grappled with the guard, trying to wrest the shotgun from him. As they struggled together by the staircase he saw that the stream had expanded into a broad sheet, as wide as the sloping floor, moving swiftly like a tidal race. It swilled below the land-cruisers and around the wheels of the burning cars, touched here and there by the nimbus of a flame. The fluid overran Stillman's feet as he and his men turned and ran for their lives, splashing through the fast-moving sluice. In the last seconds, as the whole floor lit up in a sudden bloom of flame, illuminating the running figures trapped in the centre of this sloping furnace, Halloway hurled himself down the staircase. The sounds of explosions followed him to the ground floor.

So Olds had opened the stopcocks on the fuel tanks of the cars on the ninth and tenth floors. When Halloway reached the road the upper three storeys of the garage were aflame. Powerful explosions were ripping apart the limousines, sports-cars and open tourers that Olds had collected so carefully. Window glass and pieces of sharp chrome flicked through the air, landing on the sidewalk around him as he crouched behind an airline van. Fifty feet high, the flames of the burning gasolene rose into a sluggish tower of smoke two hundred yards in diameter.

Most of Stillman's men had driven off, these youths in their black uniforms and large cars frightened by the violence of the explosions. Three others had remained behind, waiting with their rifles raised, but Halloway was certain that both Olds and Stillman had already died.

High above him, a propeller whirled through the smoke. The sailplane moved across the roof, lining itself up for take-off. Olds' slim figure was crouched in the cockpit, face hidden by the antique helmet. The engine deepened its roar, and the aircraft with its long drooping wings sped forward down the sloping roof. As it left the building and sailed into the open air it seemed to fall towards the ground, but its wings suddenly climbed on to the light wind crossing the airport. It soared along, engine blaring, a few feet above the cars parked nose-to-tail down the runway, and shook off the oily smoke that still wreathed its wings and fuselage. It flew on steadily, gaining altitude as it cleared the perimeter fence. Moving northwards towards the Sound, it made a careful left-hand turn, three hundred feet above the ground. It set off across the river, wings rocking as Olds tested the controls. Halfway across the river it picked up a flight of wild duck which were circling the city, and then joined a stream of petals half a mile long that was being carried away by the wind. Together, the three flights – the wild duck and the stream of petals, and Olds in his sailplane – flew on to the north-west, parting company when they crossed the ruined suspension bridge. Halloway waited as the sailplane, little more than a point of light reflected from its propeller, climbed higher into the secure sky, and finally vanished on its way westwards across the continent.

When he had driven back to the city Halloway left his car in the square. Standing beside Buckmaster's memorial, he watched the supermarkets and stores, the bars and amusement arcades close themselves down. Almost everyone had left now, as the young people made their way back to their garden settlements.

Halloway waited until they had all gone. The last of the generators had run out of fuel, dimming the lights in the police-station. He walked through the streets, picking his way over the broken glass and burnt-out cables, past dozens of abandoned cars. Discarded banknotes, printed with his own name, drifted along the roadway.

In the space of only a few months he had managed to achieve what had taken this metropolis as a whole more than a hundred and fifty years to do. However, it had all been worth while. He knew now that he would never return to Garden City, with its pastoral calm. In the morning, after he had rested, he would set off on foot, searching for Olds and the sailplane, following the memorials westwards across the continent, until he found the old man again and could help him raise his pyramids of washing-machines, radiator-grilles and typewriters. Somehow he would come to terms with Miranda, and help her to re-forest the cities. Maybe, then, she would wear her wedding dress again for him.

Confident of all this, Halloway set off across the square. Already he was planning the first of a series of huge metal pyramids in his mind, as high perhaps as these skyscrapers, built of airliners, freight trains, walking draglines and missile launchers, larger than anything of which Buckmaster and the Twentieth Century had ever dreamed. And perhaps, too, Olds would teach him how to fly.

Low-Flying Aircraft

'The man's playing some sort of deranged game with himself.'

From their balcony on the tenth floor of the empty hotel, Forrester and his wife watched the light aircraft taking off from the runway at Ampuriabrava, half a mile down the beach. A converted crop-sprayer with a silver fuselage and open cockpits, the biplane was lining up at the end of the concrete airstrip. Its engine blared across the deserted resort like a demented fan.

'One of these days he's not going to make it – I'm certain that's what he's waiting for ... ' Without thinking, Forrester climbed from his deck-chair and pushed past the drinks trolley to the balcony rail. The aircraft was now moving rapidly along the runway, tail-wheel still touching the tarmac marker line. Little more than two hundred feet of concrete lay in front of it. The runway had been built thirty years earlier for the well-to-do Swiss and Germans bringing their private aircraft to this vacation complex on the Costa Brava. By now, in the absence of any maintenance, the concrete pier jutting into the sea had been cut to a third of its original length by the strong offshore currents.

However, the pilot seemed unconcerned, his bony forehead exposed above his goggles, long hair tied in a brigand's knot. Forrester waited, hands gripping the rail in a confusion of emotions – he wanted to see this reclusive and stand-offish doctor plunge on to the rocks, but at the same time his complicated rivalry with Gould made him shout out a warning.

At the last moment, with a bare twenty feet of runway left, Gould sat back sharply in his seat, almost pulling the aircraft into the air. It rose steeply over the broken concrete causeway, banked and made a low circuit of the sea before setting off inland.

Forrester looked up as it crossed their heads. Sometimes he thought that Gould was deliberately trying to provoke him – or Judith, more likely. There was some kind of unstated bond that linked them.

'Did you watch the take-off?' he asked. 'There won't be many more of those.'

Judith lay back in her sun-seat, staring vaguely at the now silent airstrip. At one time Forrester had played up the element of danger in these take-offs, hoping to distract her during the last tedious months of the pregnancy. But the pantomime was no longer necessary, even today, when they were waiting for the *practicante* to bring the results of the amniotic scan from Figueras. After the next summer storm had done its worst to the crumbling runway, Gould was certain to crash. Curiously, he could have avoided all this by clearing a section of any one of a hundred abandoned roads.

'It's almost too quiet now,' Judith said. 'Have you seen the *practicante*? He was supposed to come this morning.'

'He'll be here – the clinic is only open one day a week.' Forrester took his wife's small foot and held it between his hands, openly admiring her pale legs without any guile or calculation. 'Don't worry, this time it's going to be good news.'

'I know. It's strange, but I'm absolutely certain of it too. I've never had any doubts, all these months.'

Forrester listened to the drone of the light aircraft as it disappeared above the hills behind the resort. In the street below him the sand blown up from the beach formed a series of encroaching dunes that had buried many of the cars to their windows. Fittingly, the few tyre-tracks that led to the hotel entrance all belonged to the *practicante*'s Honda. The clacking engine of this serious-faced male nurse sounded its melancholy tocsin across the town. He had tended Judith since their arrival two months earlier, with elaborate care but a total lack of emotional tone, as if he were certain already of the pregnancy's ultimate outcome.

None the less, Forrester found himself still clinging to hope. Once he had feared these fruitless pregnancies, the enforced trips from Geneva, and the endless circuit of empty Mediterranean resorts as they waited for yet another seriously deformed foetus to make its appearance. But he had looked forward to this last pregnancy, seeing it almost as a challenge, a game played against enormous odds for the greatest possible prize. When Judith had first told him, six months earlier, that she had conceived again he had immediately made arrangements for their drive to Spain. Judith conceived so easily – the paradox was bitter, this vigorous and unquenched sexuality, this enormous fertility, even if of a questionable kind, at full flood in an almost depopulated world.

'Richard – come on. You look dead. Let's drink a toast to me.' Judith pulled the trolley over to her chair. She sat up, animating herself like a toy. Seeing their reflections in the bedroom mirror, Forrester thought of their resemblance to a pair of latter-day Scott Fitzgeralds, two handsome and glamorous bodies harbouring their guilty secret.

'Do you realize that we'll know the results of the scan by this evening? Richard, we'll have to celebrate! Perhaps we should have gone to Benidorm.'

'It's a huge place,' Forrester pointed out. 'There might be fifteen or twenty people there for the summer.'

'That's what I mean. We ought to meet other people, share the good news with them.'

'Well ... ' They had come to this quiet resort at the northern end of the Costa Brava specifically to get away from everyone – in fact, Forrester had resented finding

Gould here, this hippified doctor who lived in one of the abandoned hotels on the *playa* and unexpectedly turned up in his aircraft after a weekend's absence.

Forrester surveyed the lines of deserted hotels and apartment houses, the long-shuttered rotisseries and supermarkets. There was something reassuring about the emptiness. He felt more at ease here, almost alone in this forgotten town.

As they stood together by the rail, sipping their drinks and gazing at the silent bay, Forrester held his wife around her full waist. For weeks now he had barely been able to take his hands off her. Once Gould had gone it would be pleasant here. They would lie around for the rest of the summer, making love all the time and playing with the baby – a rare arrival now, the average for normal births was less than one in a thousand. Already he could visualize a few elderly peasants coming down from the hills and holding some sort of primitive earth festival on the beach.

Behind them the aircraft had reappeared over the town. For a moment he caught sight of the doctor's silver helmet – one of Gould's irritating affectations was to paint stripes on his helmet and flying-jacket, and on the fenders of his old Mercedes, a sophomore conceit rather out of character. Forrester had come across traces of the paint at various points around the town – on the footbridge over the canal dividing the marina and airstrip at Ampuriabrava from the beach hotels in Rosas, at the corners of the streets leading to Gould's hotel. These marks, apparently made at random, were elements of a cryptic private language. For some time now Forrester had been certain that Gould was up to some nefarious game in the mountains. He was probably pillaging the abandoned monasteries, looting their icons and gold plate. Forrester had a potent vision of this solitary doctor, piloting his light aircraft in a ceaseless search of the Mediterranean littoral, building up a stockpile of art treasures in case the world opened up for business again.

Forrester's last meeting with Gould, in the Dali museum at Figueras, seemed to confirm these suspicions. He had dropped Judith off at the ante-natal clinic, where the amniotic scanning would, they hoped, confirm the absence of any abnormalities in the foetus, and by an error of judgment strolled into this museum dedicated by the town to its most illustrious native artist. As he walked quickly through the empty galleries he noticed Gould lounging back on the central divan, surveying with amiable composure the surrealist's flaccid embryos and anatomical monstrosities. With his silver-flecked jacket and long hair in a knot, Gould looked less like a doctor than a middle-aged Hell's Angel. Beside him on the divan were three canvases he had selected from the walls, and which he later took back to decorate his hotel rooms.

'They're a little too close to the knuckle for me,' Forrester commented. 'A collection of newsreels from Hell.'

'A sharp guess at the future, all right,' Gould agreed. 'The ultimate dystopia is the inside of one's own head.'

As they left the museum Forrester said, 'Judith's baby is due in about three weeks. We wondered if you'd care to attend her?'

Gould made no reply. Shifting the canvases from one arm to the other, he scowled at the trees in the deserted *rambla*. His eyes seemed to be waiting for something. Not for the first time, Forrester realized how tired the man was, the nervousness underlying his bony features.

'What about the *practicante*? He's probably better qualified than I am.'

'I wasn't thinking of the birth, so much, as the ... '

'As the death?'

'Well ... ' Unsettled by Gould's combative tone, Forrester searched through his stock of euphemisms. 'We're full of hope, of course, but we've had to learn to be realistic.'

'That's admirable of you both.'

'Given one possible outcome, I think Judith would prefer someone like you to deal with it ... '

Gould was nodding sagely at this. He looked sharply at Forrester. 'Why not keep the child? Whatever the outcome.'

Forrester had been genuinely shocked by this. Surprised by the doctor's aggression, he watched him swing away with an unpleasant gesture, the lurid paintings under his arm, and stride back to his Mercedes.

Judith was asleep in the bedroom. From her loose palm Forrester removed the Valiums she had been too tired to take. He replaced them in the capsule, and then sat unsteadily on the bed. For the last hour he had been drinking alone in the sun on the balcony, partly out of boredom – the time-scale of the human pregnancy was a major evolutionary blunder, he decided – and partly out of confused fear and hope.

Where the hell was the *practicante*? Forrester walked on to the balcony again and scanned the road to Figueras, past the abandoned night-clubs and motor-boat rental offices. The aircraft had gone, disappearing into the mountains. As he searched the airstrip Forrester noticed the dark-robed figure of a young woman in the doorway of Gould's hangar. He had seen her mooning around there several times before, and openly admitted to himself that he felt a slight pang of envy at the assumed sexual liaison between her and Gould. There was something secretive about the relationship that intrigued him. Careful not to move, he waited for the young woman to step into the sun. Already, thanks to the alcohol and an over-scrupulous monogamy, he could feel his loins thickening. For all his need to be alone, the thought that there was another young woman within half a mile of him almost derailed Forrester's mind.

Five minutes later he saw the girl again, standing on

the observation roof of the Club Náutico, gazing inland as if waiting for Gould's silver aircraft to return.

As Forrester let himself out of the suite his wife was still asleep. Only two of the suites on the tenth floor were now maintained. The other rooms had been locked and shuttered, time capsules that contained their melancholy cargo, the aerosols, douche-bags, hairpins and sun-oil tubes left behind by the thousands of vanished tourists.

The waiters' service elevator, powered by a small gasolene engine in the basement, carried him down to the lobby. There was no electric current now to run the air-conditioning system, but the hotel was cool. In the two basketwork chairs by the steps, below the postcard rack with its peeling holiday views of Rosas in its tourist heyday, sat the elderly manager and his wife. Señor Cervera had been a linotype operator for a Barcelona newspaper during the years when the population slide had first revealed itself, and even now was a mine of information about the world-wide decline.

'Mrs Forrester is asleep – if the *practicante* comes send him up to her.'

'I hope it's good news. You've waited a long time.'

'If it is we'll certainly celebrate tonight. Judith wants to open up all the night-clubs.'

Forrester walked into the sunlight, climbing over the first of the dunes that filled the street. He stood on the roof of a submerged car and looked at the line of empty hotels. He had come here once as a child, when the resort was still half-filled with tourists. Already, though, many of the hotels were closing, but his parents had told him that thirty years earlier the town had been so crowded that they could barely see the sand on the beach. Forrester could remember the Club Náutico, presiding like an aircraft-carrier over the bars and night-clubs of Ampuriabrava, packed with people enjoying themselves with a frantic *fin de siècle* gaiety. Already the first of the so-called

'Venus hotels' were being built, and coachloads of deranged young couples were coming in from the airport at Gerona.

Forrester jumped from the roof of the car and set off along the beach road towards Ampuriabrava. The immaculate sand ran down to the water, free at last of cigarette-ends and bottle-tops, as clean and soft as milled bone. As he moved past the empty hotels it struck Forrester as strange that he felt no sense of panic at the thought of these vanished people. Like Judith and everyone else he knew, like the old linotype operator and his wife sitting alone in the lobby of their hotel, he calmly accepted the terrifying logic of this reductive nightmare as if it were a wholly natural and peaceful event.

Forty years earlier, by contrast, there had been an uncontrolled epidemic of fear as everyone became aware of the marked fall in the world's population, the huge apparent drop in the birth-rate and, even more disquieting, the immense increase in the number of deformed foetuses. Whatever had set off this process, which now left Forrester standing alone on this once-crowded Costa Brava beach, the results were dramatic and irreversible. At its present rate of decline Europe's population of 200,000 people, and the United States' population of 150,000, were headed for oblivion within a generation.

At the same time, by an unhappy paradox, there had been no fall in fertility, either in man or in the few animal species also affected. In fact, birth-rates had soared, but almost all the offspring were seriously deformed. Forrester remembered the first of Judith's children, with their defective eyes, in which the optic nerves were exposed, and even more disturbing, their deformed sexual organs – these grim parodies of human genitalia tapped all kinds of nervousness and loathing.

Forrester stopped at the end of the beach, where the line of hotels turned at right angles along the entrance channel of the marina. Looking back at the town, he realized that he was almost certainly its last visitor. The continued breakdown of the European road-systems would soon rule out any future journeys to Spain. For the past five years he and Judith had lived in Geneva. Working for a United Nations agency, he moved from city to city across Europe, in charge of a team making inventories of the huge stockpiles of foodstuffs, pharmaceuticals, consumer durables and industrial raw materials that lay about in warehouses and rail terminals, in empty supermarkets and stalled production-lines – enough merchandise to keep the dwindling population going for a thousand years. Although the population of Geneva was some two thousand, most of Europe's urban areas were deserted altogether, including, surprisingly, some of its great cathedral cities – Chartres, Cologne and Canterbury were empty shells. For some reason the consolations of religion meant nothing to anyone. On the other hand, despite the initial panic, there had never been any real despair. For thirty years they had been matter-of-factly slaughtering their children and closing down the western hemisphere like a group of circus workers dismantling their tents and killing their animals at the season's end.

From the bank of the canal Forrester peered up at the white hull of the Club Náutico. There were no signs of the young woman. Behind him, facing the airstrip, was a roadside restaurant abandoned years before. Through the salt-stained windows he could see the rows of bottles against the mirror behind the bar, chairs stacked on tables.

Forrester pushed back the door. The interior of the restaurant was like a museum tableau. Nothing had been moved for years. Despite the unlocked door there had been no vandalism. From the footprints visible in the fine sand blown across the floor it was clear that over the years a few passing travellers had refreshed themselves at the bar and left without doing any damage. This was true of everywhere Forrester had visited. They had vacated a hundred cities and airports as if leaving them in serviceable condition for their successors.

The air in the restaurant was stale but cool. Seated behind the bar, Forrester helped himself to a bottle of Fundador, drinking quietly as he waited for the young woman to reappear. As he gazed across the canal he noticed that Gould had painted two continuous marker lines in fluorescent silver across the metal slats and wire railing of the footbridge. From the door he could see the same marker lines crossing the road and climbing the steps to Gould's hotel, where they disappeared into the lobby.

Standing unsteadily in the road, Forrester frowned up at the garish façade of the hotel, which had been designed in a crudely erotic Graecian style. Naked caryatids three storeys high supported a sham portico emblazoned with satyrs and nymphs. Why had Gould chosen to live in this hotel, out of all those standing empty in Rosas? Here in what amounted to the red-light quarter of the town, it was one of a group known euphemistically all over the world as the 'Venus hotels', but which Judith more accurately referred to as 'the sex-hotels'. From Waikiki to Glyfada Beach, Rio to Recife, these hotel complexes had sprung up in the first years of the depopulation crisis. A flood of government-subsidised tourists had poured in, urged on into a last frantic festival of erotomania. In a misguided attempt to rekindle their fertility, every conceivable kind of deviant sexual activity had been encouraged. Pornographic hotel decor, lobbies crammed with aids and appliances, ceaseless sex-films shown on closed-circuit television, all these reflected an unhappy awareness by everyone that their sex no longer mattered. The sense of obligation, however residual, to a future generation was no longer present. If anything, the 'normal' had become the real obscenity. In the foyer of one of these hotels Forrester and Judith had come across the most sinister pornographic image of all – the photograph of a healthy baby obscenely retouched.

7

Judith and her husband had been too young to take part in these despairing orgies, and by the time of their marriage there had been a general revulsion against perverse sex of every kind. Chastity and romantic love, pre-marital celibacy and all the restraints of monogamy came back in force. As the world's populations continued to fall, the last married couples sat dutifully together like characters from a Vermeer interior.

And all the while the sexual drive continued unabated. Feeling the alcohol surge through him, Forrester swayed through the hot sunlight. Somewhere around the hangar beside the airstrip the young woman was waiting for him, perhaps watching him at this moment from its dark interior. Obviously she knew what he was thinking, and almost seemed to be encouraging him with her flirtatious dartings to and fro.

Forrester stepped on to the bridge. Behind him the line of garish hotels was silent, a stage-set designed for just this adventure. The metal rungs of the bridge rang softly under his feet. Tapping them like the keys of a xylophone, Forrester stumbled against the rail, smearing his hands against the still-wet stripe of silver paint.

Without thinking, he wiped his hands on his shirt. The lines of fluorescent paint continued across the bridge, winding in and out of the abandoned cars in the parking lot beside the airstrip. Following Gould's illuminated pathway, Forrester crossed the canal. When he reached the fuel store he saw that the young woman had emerged from the hangar. She stood in the open doorway, her feet well within the rectangle of sunlight. Her intelligent but somehow mongoloid face was hidden as usual behind heavy sunglasses – a squat chin and high forehead fronted by a carapace of black glass. For all this concealment, Forrester was certain that she had been expecting him, and even more that she had been hoping for him to appear. Inside her black shawl she was moving her hands about like a schoolgirl – no doubt she was aware that he was the only man in the resort, apart from Gould, away on his endless solo flying, and the old linotype operator.

The sweat rose from Forrester's skin, a hot pelt across his forehead. Standing beside the fuel hydrant, he wiped away the sweat with his hands. The young woman seemed to respond to these gestures. Her own hands emerged from the shawl, moving about in a complex code, a semaphore signalling Forrester to her. Responding in turn, he touched his face again, ignoring the silver paint on his hands. As if to ingratiate himself, he smeared the last of the paint over his cheeks and nose, wiping the tacky metal stains across his mouth.

When he reached the young woman and touched her shoulder she looked with sudden alarm at these luminous contours, as if aware that she had been forming the elements of the wrong man from these painted fragments—his hands, chest and features.

Too late, she let herself be bundled backwards into the darkness of the hangar. The sunglasses fell from her hands to the floor. Forrester's luminous face shone back at him like a chromiumed mask from the flight-office windows. He looked down at the sightless young woman scrabbling at his feet for her sunglasses, one hand trying to hide her eyes from him. Then he heard the drone of a light aircraft flying over the town.

Gould's aircraft circled the Club Náutico, the panels of its silver fuselage reflecting the sun like a faceted mirror. Forrester turned from the young woman lying against the rear wall of the hangar, the glasses with their fractured lenses once more over her face. He stepped into the afternoon light and ran across the runway as the aircraft came in to land.

Two hours later, when he had crossed the deserted streets to his hotel, he found Señor Cervera standing on the dune below the steps, hands cupped to his eyes. He waved Forrester towards him, greeting him with relief.

Forrester had spent the interval in one of the hotels in the centre of Rosas, moving restlessly from one bathroom to the next as he tried to clean the paint off his face and hands. He had slept for half an hour in a bedroom.

'Mrs Forrester – ' The old man gestured helplessly.

'Where is she?' Forrester followed Cervera to the hotel steps. His wife was hovering in an embarrassed way behind her mahogany desk. 'What's happened?'

'The *practicante* arrived – just after you left.' The old man paused to examine the traces of silver paint that still covered Forrester's face. With a wave of the hand, as if dismissing them as another minor detail of this aberrant day, he said, 'He brought the result to Mrs Forrester ... '

'Is she all right? What's going on?'

Forrester started towards the elevator but the old woman waved him back. 'She went out – I tried to stop her. She was all dressed up.'

'Dressed? How?'

'In ... in a very extravagant way. She was upset.'

'Oh, my God ... ' Forrester caught his breath. 'Poor Judith – where did she go?'

'To the hotels.' Cervera raised a hand and pointed reluctantly towards the Venus hotels.

Forrester found her within half an hour, in the bridal suite on the third floor of one of the hotels. As he ran along the canal road, shouting out Judith's name, Gould was walking slowly across the footbridge, flying helmet in hand. The dark figure of the young woman, the lenses of her fractured sunglasses like black suns, followed him sightlessly from the door of the hangar as Gould moved along the painted corridor.

When at last he heard Judith's cry Forrester entered the hotel. In the principal suite on the third floor he discovered her stretched out on the bridal bed, surrounded by the obscene murals and bas-reliefs. She lay back on the dusty lamé bedspread, dressed in a whore's finery she had put together from her own wardrobe. Like a drunken courtesan in the last hours of pregnancy, she stared glassily at Forrester as if not wanting to recognize him. As he approached she picked up the harness beside her on the bed and tried to strike him with it. Forrester pulled it from her hands. He held her shoulders, hoping to calm her, but his feet slipped in the vibrators and film cassettes strewn about the bed. When he regained his balance Judith was at the door. He ran after her down the corridor, kicking aside the display stands of pornographic magazines outside each bedroom. Judith was fleeing down the staircase, stripping off pieces of her costume. Then, thankfully, he saw Gould waiting for her on the landing below, arms raised to catch her.

At dusk, when Gould and Forrester had taken the distraught woman back to the hotel, the two men stood by the entrance in the dusk.

In an unexpected gesture of concern, Gould touched Forrester's shoulder. Apart from this, his face remained without expression. 'She'll sleep till morning. Ask the *practicante* to give you some thalidomide for her. You'll need to sedate her through the next three weeks.'

He pointed to the silver stains on Forrester's face. 'These days we're all wearing our war-paint. You were over at the hangar, just before I landed. Carmen told me that you'd accidentally stepped on her glasses.'

Relieved that the young woman, for whatever reasons, had not betrayed him, Forrester said, 'I was trying to reassure her–she seemed to be worried that you were overdue.'

'I'm having to fly further inland now. She's nervous when I'm not around.'

'I hadn't realized that she was ... blind,' Forrester said as they walked down the street towards the canal. 'It's good of you to look after her. The Spaniards would kill her out of hand if they found her here. What happens when you leave?'

'She'll be all right, by then.' Gould stopped and gazed through the fading light at the causeway of the airstrip. A section of the porous concrete seemed to have collapsed into the sea. Gould nodded to himself, as if working out the time left to him by this fragmenting pier. 'Now, what about this baby?'

'It's another one – the same defects. I'll get the *practicante* to deal with it.'

'Why?' Before Forrester could reply, Gould took his arm. 'Forrester, it's a fair question. Which of us can really decide who has the defects?'

'The mothers seem to know.'

'But are they right? I'm beginning to think that a massacre of the innocents has taken place that literally out-Herods Herod. Look, come up with me tomorrow – the Cerveras can look after your wife, she'll sleep all day. You'll find it an interesting flight.'

They took off at ten o'clock the following morning. Sitting in the front cockpit, with the draught from the propeller full in his face, Forrester was convinced that they would crash. At full throttle they moved swiftly along the runway, the freshly broken concrete slabs already visible. Forrester looked over his shoulder, hoping that Gould would somehow manage to stop the aircraft before they were killed, but the doctor's face was hidden behind his goggles, as if he was unaware of the danger. At the last moment, when the cataract of concrete blocks was almost below the wheels, Gould pulled back on the stick. The small aircraft rose steeply, as if jerked into the air by a huge hand. Thirty seconds later Forrester began to breathe.

They levelled out and made a left-hand circuit of the empty resort. Already Gould was pointing with a gloved hand at the patches of phosphorescent paint in the hills above Rosas. Before the take-off, while Forrester sat uncomfortably in the cockpit, wondering why he had accepted this challenge, the young woman had wheeled a drum of liquid over to the aircraft. Gould pumped the contents into the tank which Forrester could see below his feet. As he waited, the young woman walked round to the cockpit and stared up at Forrester, clearly hoping to see something in his face. There was something grotesque, almost comic, about this mongoloid girl surveying the world with her defunct vision through these cracked sunglasses. Perhaps she was disappointed that he was no longer interested in her. Forrester turned away from her sightless stare, thinking of Judith asleep in the darkened hotel room, and the small and unwelcome tenant of her body.

Eight hundred feet below them was a wide valley that led inland towards the foothills of the Pyrenees. The line of low mountains marked the northern wall of the plain of Ampurdan, a rich farming area where even now there were small areas of cultivation. But all the cattle had gone, slaughtered years beforehand.

As they followed the course of the valley, Forrester could see that sections of the pathways and farm tracks which climbed the hills had been sprayed with phosphorescent paint. Panels of silver criss-crossed the sides of the valley.

So this was what Gould had been doing on his flights, painting sections of the mountainside in a huge pop-art display. The doctor was waving down at the valley floor, where a small, shaggy-haired bullock, like a miniature bison, stood in an apparent daze on an isolated promontory. Cutting back the engine, Gould banked the aircraft and flew low over the valley floor, not more than twenty feet above the creature. Forrester was speculating on how this sightless creature, clearly a mutant, had managed to survive, when there was a sudden jolt below his feet. The ventral spraying head had been lowered, and a moment later a huge gust of silver paint was vented into the air and fanned out behind them. It hung there in a luminescent cloud, and then settled to form a narrow brush-stroke down the side of the mountain. Retracting the spraying head, Gould made a steep circuit of the valley. He throttled up his engine and dived over the head of the bullock, driving it down the mountainside from its promontory. As it stumbled left and right, unable to get its bearings, it crossed the silver pathway. Immediately it gathered its legs together and set off at a brisk trot along this private roadway.

For the next hour they flew up the valley, and Forrester saw that these lines of paint sprayed from the air were part of an elaborate series of trails leading into the safety of the mountains. When they finally turned back, circling a remote gorge above a small lake, Forrester was not surprised to see that a herd of several hundred of the creatures had made their home here. Lifting their heads, they seemed to follow Gould as he flew past them. Tirelessly, he laid down more marker lines wherever they were needed, driving any errant cattle back on to the illuminated pathways.

When they landed at Ampuriabrava he waited on the runway as Gould shut down the aircraft. The young woman came out from the darkness inside the hangar, and stood with her arms folded inside her shawl. Forrester noticed that the sides of the aircraft fuselage and tailplane were a brilliant silver, bathed in the metallic spray through which they had endlessly circled. Gould's helmet and flying-suit, and his own face and shoulders, shone like mirrors, as if they had just alighted from the sun. Curiously, only their eyes, protected by their goggles, were free from the paint, dark orbits into which the young woman gazed as if hoping to find someone of her own kind.

Gould greeted her, handing her his helmet. He stripped off his flying-jacket and ushered her into the hangar.

He pointed across the canal. 'We'll have a drink in your

bar.' He led the way diagonally across the car-park, ignoring the painted pathways. 'I think there's enough on us for Carmen to know where we are. It gives her a sense of security.'

'How long have you been herding the cattle?' Forrester asked when they were seated behind the bar.

'Since the winter. Somehow one herd escaped the farmers' machetes. Flying down from Perpignan through the Col du Perthus, I noticed them following the aircraft. In some way they could see me, using a different section of the electromagnetic spectrum. Then I realized that I'd sprayed some old landing-light reflector paint on the plane – highly phosphorescent stuff.'

'But why save them? They couldn't survive on their own.'

'Not true – in fact, they're extremely hardy. By next winter they'll be able to out-run and out-think everything else around here. Like Carmen – she's a very bright girl. She's managed to keep herself going here for years, without being able to see a thing. When I started getting all this paint over me I think I was the first person she'd ever seen.'

Thinking again of Judith's baby, Forrester shook his head. 'She looks like a mongol to me – that swollen forehead.'

'You're wrong. I've found out a lot about her. She has a huge collection of watches with luminous dials, hundreds of them, that she's been filching for years from the shops. She's got them all working together but to different times, it's some sort of gigantic computer. God only knows what overlit world nature is preparing her for, but I suppose we won't be around to see it.'

Forrester gazed disagreeably into his glass of brandy. For once the Fundador made him feel ill. 'Gould, are you saying in effect that the child Judith is carrying at this moment is *not* deformed?'

Gould nodded encouragingly. 'It's not deformed at

all – any more than Carmen. It's like the so-called population decline that we've all accepted as an obvious truth. In fact, there hasn't been a decline – except in the sense that we've been slaughtering our offspring. Over the past fifty years the birth-rate has gone up, not down.' Before Forrester could protest, he went on, 'Try for a moment to retain an open mind – we have this vastly increased sexuality, and an unprecedented fertility. Even your wife has had – what – seven children. Yet why? Isn't it obvious that we were intended to embark on a huge replacement programme, though sadly the people we're replacing turn out to be ourselves. Our job is simply to repopulate the world with our successors. As for our need to be alone, this intense enjoyment of our own company, and the absence of any sense of despair, I suppose they're all nature's way of saying goodbye.'

'And the runway?' Forrester asked. 'Is that your way of saying goodbye?'

A month later, as soon as Judith had recovered from the birth of her son, she and Forrester left Rosas to return to Geneva. After they had made their farewells to Señor Cervera and his wife, Forrester drove the car along the beach road. It was 11 a.m., but Gould's aircraft still stood on the airstrip. For some reason the doctor was late.

'It's a long drive – are you going to be well enough?' he asked Judith.

'Of course – I've never felt better.' She settled herself in the seat. It seemed to Forrester that a kind of shutter had been lowered across her mind, hiding away all memories of the past months. She looked composed and relaxed again, but with the amiable and fixed expression of a display-window mannequin.

'Did you pay off the *practicante*?' she asked. 'They expect something extra for ... '

Forrester was gazing up at the façades of the Venus hotels. He remembered the evening of the birth, and the *practicante* carrying his son away from Señora Cervera. The district nurse had taken it for granted that he would be given the task of destroying the child. As Forrester stopped the Spaniard by the elevator he found himself wondering where the man would have killed it – in some alley behind the cheaper hotels at the rear of the town, or in any one of a thousand vacant bathrooms. But when Forrester had taken the child, careful not to look at its eyes, the *practicante* had not objected, only offering Forrester his surgical bag.

Forrester had declined. After the *practicante* had left, and before Señora Cervera returned to the lobby, he set off through the dark streets to the canal. He had put on again the silver jacket he had worn on the day when Gould had flown him into the mountains. As he crossed the bridge the young woman emerged from the hangar, almost invisible in her dark shawl. Forrester walked towards her, listening to the faint clicking and murmurs of the strong child. He pressed the infant into her hands and turned back to the canal, throwing away his jacket as he ran.

While they drove along the line of hotels to the Figueras road Forrester heard the sounds of the aircraft. Gould was climbing into the cockpit, about to warm up the engine before take-off.

'I never really understood him,' Judith commented. 'What was he up to in the mountains?'

'I don't know – some obsession of his.'

During a brief storm two nights earlier another section of the runway had collapsed. But Forrester knew that Gould would go on flying to the end, driving his herd higher into the mountains, until they no longer needed him and the day had come to take off for the last time.

The Dead Astronaut

Cape Kennedy has gone now, its gantries rising from the deserted dunes. Sand has come in across the Banana River, filling the creeks and turning the old space complex into a wilderness of swamps and broken concrete. In the summer, hunters build their blinds in the wrecked staff-cars; but by early November, when Judith and I arrived, the entire area was abandoned. Beyond Cocoa Beach, where I stopped the car, the ruined motels were half hidden in the saw grass. The launching towers rose into the evening air like the rusting ciphers of some forgotten algebra of the sky.

'The perimeter fence is half a mile ahead,' I said. 'We'll wait here until it's dark. Do you feel better now?'

Judith was staring at an immense funnel of cerise cloud that seemed to draw the day with it below the horizon, taking the light from her faded blonde hair. The previous afternoon, in the hotel in Tampa, she had fallen ill briefly with some unspecified complaint.

'What about the money?' she asked. 'They may want more, now that we're here.'

'Five thousand dollars? Ample, Judith. These relic hunters are a dying breed – few people are interested in Cape Kennedy any longer. What's the matter?'

Her thin fingers were fretting at the collar of her suede jacket. 'I ... it's just that perhaps I should have worn black.'

'Why? Judith, this isn't a funeral. For heaven's sake, Robert died twenty years ago. I know all he meant to us, but ... '

Judith was staring at the debris of tyres and abandoned cars, her pale eyes becalmed in her drawn face. 'Philip, don't you understand, he's coming back now. Someone's got to be here. The memorial service over the radio was a horrible travesty – my God, that priest would have had a shock if Robert had talked back to him. There ought to be a full-scale committee, not just you and I and these empty night-clubs.'

In a firmer voice, I said: 'Judith, there would be a committee – *if* we told the NASA Foundation what we know. The remains would be interred in the NASA vault at Arlington, there'd be a band – even the President might be there. There's still time.'

I waited for her to reply, but she was watching the gantries fade into the night sky. Fifteen years ago, when the dead astronaut orbiting the earth in his burned-out capsule had been forgotten, Judith had constituted herself a memorial committee of one. Perhaps, in a few days, when she finally held the last relics of Robert Hamilton's body in her own hands, she would come to terms with her obsession.

'Philip, over there! Is that –'

High in the western sky, between the constellations Cepheus and Cassiopeia, a point of white light moved towards us, like a lost star searching for its zodiac. Within a few minutes, it passed overhead, its faint beacon setting behind the cirrus over the sea.

'It's all right, Judith.' I showed her the trajectory timetables pencilled into my diary. 'The relic hunters read these orbits off the sky better than any computer. They must have been watching the pathways for years.'

'Who was it?'

'A Russian woman pilot – Valentina Prokrovna. She was sent up from a site near the Urals twenty-five years ago to work on a television relay system.'

'Television? I hope they enjoyed the programme.'

This callous remark, uttered by Judith as she stepped

from the car, made me realize once again her special motives for coming to Cape Kennedy. I watched the capsule of the dead woman disappear over the dark Atlantic stream, as always moved by the tragic but serene spectacle of one of these ghostly voyagers coming back after so many years from the tideways of space. All I knew of this dead Russian was her code name: Seagull. Yet, for some reason, I was glad to be there as she came down. Judith, on the other hand, felt nothing of this. During all the years she had sat in the garden in the cold evenings, too tired to bring herself to bed, she had been sustained by her concern for one only of the twelve dead astronauts orbiting the night sky.

As she waited, her back to the sea, I drove the car into the garage of an abandoned night-club fifty yards from the road. From the trunk I took out two suitcases. One, a light travel-case, contained clothes for Judith and myself. The other, fitted with a foil inlay, reinforcing straps and a second handle, was empty.

We set off north towards the perimeter fence, like two late visitors arriving at a resort abandoned years earlier.

It was twenty years now since the last rockets had left their launching platforms at Cape Kennedy. At the time, NASA had already moved Judith and me—I was a senior flight-programmer—to the great new Planetary Space Complex in New Mexico. Shortly after our arrival, we had met one of the trainee astronauts, Robert Hamilton. After two decades, all I could remember of this over-polite but sharp-eyed young man was his albino skin, so like Judith's pale eyes and opal hair, the same cold gene that crossed them both with its arctic pallor. We had been close friends for barely six weeks. Judith's infatuation was one of those confused sexual impulses that well-brought-up young women express in their own naive way; and as I watched them swim and play tennis together, I felt not so much resentful as concerned to sustain the whole passing illusion for her.

A year later, Robert Hamilton was dead. He had returned to Cape Kennedy for the last military flights before the launching grounds were closed. Three hours after lift-off, a freak meteorite collision ruptured his oxygen support system. He had lived on in his suit for another five hours. Although calm at first, his last radio transmissions were an incoherent babble Judith and I had never been allowed to hear.

A dozen astronauts had died in orbital accidents, their capsules left to revolve through the night sky like the stars of a new constellation; and at first, Judith had shown little response. Later, after her miscarriage, the figure of this dead astronaut circling the sky above us re-emerged in her mind as an obsession with time. For hours, she would stare at the bedroom clock, as if waiting for something to happen.

Five years later, after I resigned from NASA, we made our first trip to Cape Kennedy. A few military units still guarded the derelict gantries, but already the former launching site was being used as a satellite graveyard. As the dead capsules lost orbital velocity, they homed on to the master radio beacon. As well as the American vehicles, Russian and French satellites in the joint Euro-American space projects were brought down here, the burned-out hulks of the capsules exploding across the cracked concrete.

Already, too, the relic hunters were at Cape Kennedy, scouring the burning saw grass for instrument panels and flying suits and–most valuable of all–the mummified corpses of the dead astronauts.

These blackened fragments of collar-bone and shin, kneecap and rib, were the unique relics of the space age, as treasured as the saintly bones of medieval shrines. After the first fatal accident in space, public outcry demanded that these orbiting biers be brought down to earth. Unfortunately, when a returning moon rocket crashed into the Kalahari Desert, aboriginal tribesmen broke into the vehicle. Believing the crew to be dead gods, they cut off the eight hands and vanished into the bush. It had taken two years to track them down. From then on, the capsules were left in orbit to burn out on re-entry.

Whatever remains survived the crash landings in the satellite graveyard were scavenged by the relic hunters of Cape Kennedy. This band of nomads had lived for years in the wrecked cars and motels, stealing their icons under the feet of the wardens who patrolled the concrete decks. In early October, when a former NASA colleague told me that Robert Hamilton's satellite was becoming unstable, I drove down to Tampa and began to inquire about the purchase price of Robert's mortal remains. Five thousand dollars was a small price to pay for laying his ghost to rest in Judith's mind.

Eight hundred yards from the road, we crossed the perimeter fence. Crushed by the dunes, long sections of the twenty-foot-high palisade had collapsed, the saw grass growing through the steel mesh. Below us, the boundary road passed a derelict guardhouse and divided into two paved tracks. As we waited at this rendezvous, the headlamps of the wardens' half-tracks flared across the gantries near the beach.

Five minutes later, a small dark-faced man climbed from the rear seat of a car buried in the sand fifty yards away. Head down, he scuttled over to us.

'Mr and Mrs Groves?' After a pause to peer into our faces, he introduced himself tersely: 'Quinton. Sam Quinton.'

As he shook hands, his clawlike fingers examined the bones of my wrist and forearm. His sharp nose made circles in the air. He had the eyes of a nervous bird, forever searching the dunes and the grass. An Army webbing belt hung around his patched black denims. He moved his hands restlessly in the air, as if conducting a chamber ensemble hidden behind the sand hills, and I noticed his badly scarred palms. Huge weals formed pale stars in the darkness.

For a moment, he seemed disappointed by us, almost reluctant to move on. Then he set off at a brisk pace across the dunes, now and then leaving us to blunder about helplessly. Half an hour later, when we entered a shallow basin near a farm of alkali-settling beds, Judith and I were exhausted, dragging the suitcases over the broken tyres and barbed wire.

A group of cabins had been dismantled from their original sites along the beach and re-erected in the basin. Isolated rooms tilted on the sloping sand, mantelpieces and flowered paper decorating the outer walls.

The basin was full of salvaged space material: sections of capsules, heat shields, antennas and parachute canisters. Near the dented hull of a weather satellite, two sallow-faced men in sheepskin jackets sat on a car seat. The older wore a frayed Air Force cap over his eyes. With his scarred hands, he was polishing the steel visor of a space helmet. The other, a young man with a faint beard hiding his mouth, watched us approach with the detached and neutral gaze of an undertaker.

We entered the largest of the cabins, two rooms taken off the rear of a beachhouse. Quinton lit a paraffin lamp. He pointed around the dingy interior. 'You'll be ... comfortable,' he said without conviction. As Judith stared at him with unconcealed distaste, he added pointedly: 'We don't get many visitors.'

I put the suitcases on the metal bed. Judith walked into the kitchen and Quinton began to open the empty case.

'It's in here?'

I took the two packets of $100 bills from my jacket. When I had handed them to him, I said: 'The suitcase is for the ... remains. Is it big enough?'

Quinton peered at me through the ruby light, as if baffled by our presence there. 'You could have spared yourself the trouble. They've been up there a long time, Mr Groves. After the impact' – for some reason, he cast a lewd eye in Judith's direction – 'there might be enough for a chess set.'

When he had gone, I went into the kitchen. Judith stood by the stove, hands on a carton of canned food. She was staring through the window at the metal salvage, refuse of the sky that still carried Robert Hamilton in its rusty centrifuge. For a moment, I had the feeling that the entire landscape of the earth was covered with rubbish and that here, at Cape Kennedy, we had found its source.

I held her shoulders. 'Judith, is there any point in this? Why don't we go back to Tampa? I could drive here in ten days' time when it's all over –'

She turned from me, her hands rubbing the suede where I had marked it. 'Philip, I want to be here – no matter how unpleasant. Can't you understand?'

At midnight, when I finished making a small meal for us, she was standing on the concrete wall of the settling tank. The three relic hunters sitting on their car seats watched her without moving, scarred hands like flames in the darkness.

At three o'clock that morning, as we lay awake on the narrow bed, Valentina Prokrovna came down from the sky. Enthroned on a bier of burning aluminium three hundred yards wide, she soared past on her final orbit. When I went out into the night air, the relic hunters had gone. From the rim of the settling tank, I watched them race away among the dunes, leaping like hares over the tyres and wire.

I went back to the cabin. 'Judith, she's coming down. Do you want to watch?'

Her blonde hair tied within a white towel, Judith lay on the bed, staring at the cracked plasterboard ceiling. Shortly after four o'clock, as I sat beside her, a phosphorescent light filled the hollow. There was the distant sound of explosions, muffled by the high wall of the dunes. Lights flared, followed by the noise of engines and sirens.

At dawn the relic hunters returned, hands wrapped in makeshift bandages, dragging their booty with them.

After this melancholy rehearsal, Judith entered a period of sudden and unexpected activity. As if preparing the cabin for some visitor, she rehung the curtains and swept out the two rooms with meticulous care, even bringing herself to ask Quinton for a bottle of cleanser. For hours she sat at the dressing-table, brushing and shaping her hair, trying out first one style and then another. I watched her feel the hollows of her cheeks, searching for the contours of a face that had vanished twenty years ago. As she spoke about Robert Hamilton, she almost seemed worried that she would appear old to him. At other times, she referred to Robert as if he were a child, the son she and I had never been able to conceive since her miscarriage. These different roles followed one another like scenes in some private psychodrama. However, without knowing it, for years Judith and I had used Robert Hamilton for our own reasons. Waiting for him to land, and well aware that after this Judith would have no one to turn to except myself, I said nothing.

Meanwhile, the relic hunters worked on the fragments of Valentina Prokrovna's capsule: the blistered heat shield, the chassis of the radiotelemetry unit and several cans of film that recorded her collision and act of death (these, if still intact, would fetch the highest prices, films of horrific and dreamlike violence played in the underground cinemas of Los Angeles, London and Moscow). Passing the next cabin, I saw a tattered silver space-suit spread-eagled on two automobile seats. Quinton and the relic hunters knelt beside it, their arms deep inside the legs and sleeves, gazing at me with the rapt and sensitive eyes of jewellers.

An hour before dawn, I was awakened by the sound of engines along the beach. In the darkness, the three relic hunters crouched by the settling tank, their pinched faces lit by the headlamps. A long convoy of trucks and half-tracks was moving into the launching ground. Soldiers jumped down from the tailboards, unloading tents and supplies.

'What are they doing?' I asked Quinton. 'Are they looking for us?'

The old man cupped a scarred hand over his eyes. 'It's the Army,' he said uncertainly. 'Manoeuvres, maybe. They haven't been here before like this.'

'What about Hamilton?' I gripped his bony arm. 'Are you sure –'

He pushed me away with a show of nervous temper. 'We'll get him first. Don't worry, he'll be coming sooner than they think.'

Two nights later, as Quinton prophesied, Robert Hamilton began his final descent. From the dunes near the settling tanks, we watched him emerge from the stars on his last run. Reflected in the windows of the buried cars, a thousand images of the capsule flared in the saw grass around us. Behind the satellite, a wide fan of silver spray opened in a phantom wake.

In the Army encampment by the gantries, there was a surge of activity. A blaze of headlamps crossed the concrete lanes. Since the arrival of these military units, it had become plain to me, if not to Quinton, that far from being on manoeuvres, they were preparing for the landing of Robert Hamilton's capsule. A dozen half-tracks had been churning around the dunes, setting fire to the abandoned cabins and crushing the old car bodies. Platoons of soldiers were repairing the perimeter fence and replacing the sections of metalled road that the relic hunters had dismantled.

Shortly after midnight, at an elevation of forty-two

degrees in the north-west, between Lyra and Hercules, Robert Hamilton appeared for the last time. As Judith stood up and shouted into the night air, an immense blade of light cleft the sky. The expanding corona sped towards us like a gigantic signal flare, illuminating every fragment of the landscape.

'Mrs Groves!' Quinton darted after Judith and pulled her down into the grass as she ran towards the approaching satellite. Three hundred yards away, the silhouette of a half-track stood out on an isolated dune, its feeble spotlights drowned by the glare.

With a low metallic sigh, the burning capsule of the dead astronaut soared over our heads, the vaporizing metal pouring from its hull. A few seconds later, as I shielded my eyes, an explosion of detonating sand rose from the ground behind me. A curtain of dust lifted into the darkening air like a vast spectre of powdered bone. The sounds of the impact rolled across the dunes. Near the launching gantries, fires flickered where fragments of the capsule had landed. A pall of phosphorescing gas hung in the air, particles within it beading and winking.

Judith had gone, running after the relic hunters through the swerving spotlights. When I caught up with them, the last fires of the explosion were dying among the gantries. The capsule had landed near the old Atlas launching pads, forming a shallow crater fifty yards in diameter. The slopes were scattered with glowing particles, sparkling like fading eyes. Judith ran distraughtly up and down, searching the fragments of smouldering metal.

Someone struck my shoulder. Quinton and his men, hot ash on their scarred hands, ran past like a troop of madmen, eyes wild in the crazed night. As we darted away through the flaring spotlights, I looked back at the beach. The gantries were enveloped in a pale-silver sheen that hovered there, and then moved away like a dying wraith over the sea.

At dawn, as the engines growled among the dunes, we collected the last remains of Robert Hamilton. The old man came into our cabin. As Judith watched from the kitchen, drying her hands on a towel, he gave me a cardboard shoe-box.

I held the box in my hands. 'Is this all you could get?'

'It's all there was. Look at them, if you want.'

'That's all right. We'll be leaving in half an hour.'

He shook his head. 'Not now. They're all around. If you move, they'll find us.'

He waited for me to open the shoe-box, then grimaced and went out into the pale light.

We stayed for another four days, as the Army patrols searched the surrounding dunes. Day and night, the half-tracks lumbered among the wrecked cars and cabins. Once, as I watched with Quinton from a fallen water tower, a half-track and two jeeps came within four hundred yards of the basin, held back only by the stench from the settling beds and the cracked concrete causeways.

During this time, Judith sat in the cabin, the shoe-box on her lap. She said nothing to me, as if she had lost all interest in me and the salvage-filled hollow at Cape Kennedy. Mechanically, she combed her hair, making and remaking her face.

On the second day, I came in after helping Quinton bury the cabins to their windows in the sand. Judith was standing by the table.

The shoe-box was open. In the centre of the table lay a pile of charred sticks, as if she had tried to light a small fire. Then I realized what was there. As she stirred the ash with her fingers, grey flakes fell from the joints, revealing the bony points of a clutch of ribs, a right hand and shoulder blade.

She looked at me with puzzled eyes. 'They're black,' she said.

Holding her in my arms, I lay with her on the bed. A

loudspeaker reverberated among the dunes, fragments of the amplified commands drumming at the panes.

When they moved away, Judith said: 'We can go now.'

'In a little while, when it's clear. What about these?'

'Bury them. Anywhere, it doesn't matter.' She seemed calm at last, giving me a brief smile, as if to agree that this grim charade was at last over.

Yet, when I had packed the bones into the shoe-box, scraping up Robert Hamilton's ash with a dessertspoon, she kept it with her, carrying it into the kitchen while she prepared our meals.

It was on the third day that we fell ill.

After a long, noise-filled night, I found Judith sitting in front of the mirror, combing thick clumps of hair from her scalp. Her mouth was open, as if her lips were stained with acid. As she dusted the loose hair from her lap, I was struck by the leprous whiteness of her face.

Standing up with an effort, I walked listlessly into the kitchen and stared at the saucepan of cold coffee. A sense of indefinable exhaustion had come over me, as if the bones in my body had softened and lost their rigidity. On the lapels of my jacket, loose hair lay like spinning waste.

'Philip ... ' Judith swayed towards me. 'Do you feel – What is it?'

'The water.' I poured the coffee into the sink and massaged my throat. 'It must be fouled.'

'Can we leave?' She put a hand up to her forehead. Her brittle nails brought down a handful of frayed ash hair. 'Philip, for God's sake – I'm losing all my hair!'

Neither of us was able to eat. After forcing myself through a few slices of cold meat, I went out and vomited behind the cabin.

Quinton and his men were crouched by the wall of the settling tank. As I walked toward them, steadying myself against the hull of the weather satellite, Quinton came down. When I told him that the water supplies were contaminated, he stared at me with his hard bird's eyes.

Half an hour later, they were gone.

The next day, our last there, we were worse. Judith lay on the bed, shivering in her jacket, the shoe-box held in one hand. I spent hours searching for fresh water in the cabins. Exhausted, I could barely cross the sandy basin. The Army patrols were closer. By now, I could hear the hard gear-changes of the half-tracks. The sounds from the loudspeakers drummed like fists on my head.

Then, as I looked down at Judith from the cabin doorway, a few words stuck for a moment in my mind.

'*... contaminated area ... evacuate ... radioactive ...*'

I walked forward and pulled the box from Judith's hands.

'Philip ... ' She looked up at me weakly. 'Give it back to me.'

Her face was a puffy mask. On her wrists, white flecks were forming. Her left hand reached towards me like the claw of a cadaver.

I shook the box with blunted anger. The bones rattled inside. 'For God's sake, it's *this*! Don't you see—why we're ill?'

'Philip—where are the others? The old man. Get them to help you.'

'They've gone. They went yesterday, I told you.' I let the box fall on to the table. The lid broke off, spilling the ribs tied together like a bundle of firewood. 'Quinton knew what was happening—why the Army is here. They're trying to warn us.'

'What do you mean?' Judith sat up, the focus of her eyes sustained only by a continuous effort. 'Don't let them take Robert. Bury him here somewhere. We'll come back later.'

'Judith!' I bent over the bed and shouted hoarsely at her. 'Don't you realize—there was a *bomb* on board! Robert Hamilton was carrying an atomic weapon!' I pulled back the curtains from the window. 'My God, what a joke. For twenty years, I put up with him because I couldn't ever be really sure ... '

'Philip ... '

'Don't worry, I used him – thinking about him was the only thing that kept us going. And all the time, he was waiting up there to pay us back!'

There was a rumble of exhaust outside. A half-track with red crosses on its doors and hood had reached the edge of the basin. Two men in vinyl suits jumped down, counters raised in front of them.

'Judith, before we go, tell me ... I never asked you –'

Judith was sitting up, touching the hair on her pillow. One half of her scalp was almost bald. She stared at her weak hands with their silvering skin. On her face was an expression I had never seen before, the dumb anger of betrayal.

As she looked at me, and at the bones scattered across the table, I knew my answer.

My Dream of Flying to Wake Island

Melville's dream of flying to Wake Island—a hopeless ambition, given all his handicaps—came alive again when he found the crashed aircraft buried in the dunes above the beach-house. Until then, during these first three months at the abandoned resort built among the sand-hills, his obsession with Wake Island had rested on little more than a collection of fraying photographs of this Pacific atoll, a few vague memories of its immense concrete runways, and an unfulfilled vision of himself at the controls of a light aircraft, flying steadily westwards across the open sea.

With the discovery of the crashed bomber in the dunes, everything had changed. Instead of spending his time wandering aimlessly along the beach, or gazing from the balcony at the endless sand-flats that stretched towards the sea at low tide, Melville now devoted all his time to digging the aircraft out of the dunes. He cancelled his evening games of chess with Dr Laing, his only neighbour at the empty resort, went to bed before the television programmes began and was up by five, dragging his spades and land-lines across the sand to the excavation site.

The activity suited Melville, distracting him from the sharp frontal migraines that had begun to affect him again. These returning memories of the prolonged ECT treatment unsettled him more than he had expected, with their unequivocal warning that in the margins of his mind the elements of a less pleasant world were waiting to reconstitute themselves. The dream of escaping to Wake Island was a compass bearing of sorts, but the discovery of the crashed aircraft gave him a chance to engage all his energies and, with luck, hold these migraine attacks at bay.

A number of wartime aircraft were buried near this empty resort. Walking across the sand-flats on what Dr Laing believed were marine-biology specimen hunts, Melville often found pieces of allied and enemy fighters shot down over the Channel. Rusting engine blocks and sections of cannon breeches emerged from the sand, somehow brought to the surface by the transits of the sea, and then subsided again without trace. During the summer weekends a few souvenir hunters and World War II enthusiasts picked over the sand, now and then finding a complete engine or wing spar. Too heavy to move, these relics were left where they lay. However, one of the weekend groups, led by a former advertising executive named Tennant, had found an intact Messerschmitt 109 a few feet below the sand half a mile along the coast. The members of the party parked their sports-cars at the bottom of the road below Melville's beach-house, and set off with elaborate pumps and lifting tackle in a reconditioned DUKW.

Melville noticed that Tennant was usually suspicious and stand-offish with any visitors who approached the Messerschmitt, but the advertising man was clearly intrigued by this solitary resident of the deserted resort who spent his time ambling through the debris on the beach. He offered Melville a chance of looking at the aircraft. They drove out across the wet sand to where the fighter lay like a winged saurian inside its galvanized-iron retaining wall a few feet below the surface of the flat. Tennant helped to lower Melville into the blackened cockpit, an experience which promptly brought on his first fugue.

Later, when Tennant and his co-workers had returned him to the beach-house, Melville sat for hours massaging his arms and hands, uneasily aware of certain complex digital skills that he wanted to forget but were beginning to reassert themselves in unexpected ways. Laing's solarium, with its dials and shutters, its capsule-like interior, unsettled him even more than the cockpit of the 109.

Impressive though the find was, the rusting hulk of the World War II fighter was insignificant beside Melville's discovery. He had been aware of the bomber, or at least of a large engineered structure, for some time. Wandering among the dunes above the beach-house during the warm afternoons, he had been too preoccupied at first with the task of settling in at the abandoned resort, and above all with doing nothing. Despite the endless hours he had spent in the hospital gymnasium, during his long recuperation after the aviation accident, he found the effort of walking through the deep sand soon exhausted him.

At this stage, too, he had other matters to think about. After arriving at the resort he had contacted Dr Laing, as instructed by the after-care officers at the hospital, expecting the physician to follow him everywhere. But whether deliberately or not, Laing had not been particularly interested in Melville, this ex-pilot who had turned up here impulsively in his expensive car and was now prowling restlessly around the solarium as if hunting for a chromium rat. Laing worked at the Science Research Council laboratory five miles inland, and clearly valued the privacy of the prefabricated solarium he had erected on the sand-bar at the southern end of the resort. He greeted Melville without comment, handed him the keys to the beach-house, and left him to it.

This lack of interest was a relief to Melville, but at the same time threw him on to himself. He had arrived with two suitcases, one filled with newly purchased and unfamiliar clothes, the other holding the hospital X-ray plates of his head and the photographs of Wake Island. The X-ray plates he passed to Dr Laing, who raised them to the light, scrutinizing these negatives of Melville's skull as if about to point out some design error in its construction. The photographs of Wake Island he returned without comment.

These illustrations of the Pacific atoll, with its vast concrete runways, he had collected over the previous months. During his convalescence at the hospital he had joined a wildlife conservation society, ostensibly in support of its campaign to save the Wake Island albatross from extinction – tens of thousands of the goony birds nested at the ends of the runways, and would rise in huge flocks into the flight-paths of airliners at take-off. Melville's real interest had been in the island itself, a World War II airbase and now refuelling point for trans-Pacific passenger jets. The combination of scuffed sand and concrete, metal shacks rusting by the runways, the total psychological reduction of this man-made landscape, seized his mind in a powerful but ambiguous way. For all its arid, oceanic isolation, the Wake Island in Melville's mind soon became a zone of intense possibility. He day-dreamed of flying there in a light aircraft, island-hopping across the Pacific. Once he touched down he knew that the migraines would go away for ever. He had been discharged from the Air Force in confused circumstances, and during his convalescence after the accident the military psychiatrists had been only too glad to play their parts in what soon turned out to be an under-rehearsed conspiracy of silence. When he told them that he had rented a house from a doctor in this abandoned resort, and intended to live there for a year on his back pay, they had been relieved to see him go, carrying away the X-ray plates of his head and the photographs of Wake Island.

'But why Wake Island?' Dr Laing asked him on their third chess evening. He pointed to the illustrations that Melville had pinned to the mantelpiece, and the technical abstracts lavishly documenting its geology, rainfall, seismology, flora and fauna. 'Why not Guam? Or Midway? Or the Hawaiian chain?'

'Midway would do, but it's a naval base now – I doubt if they'll give me landing clearance. Anyway, the atmosphere is wrong.' Discussing the rival merits of various Pacific islands always animated Melville, feeding this potent remythologizing of himself. 'Guam is forty miles long, covered with mountains and dense jungle, New Guinea in miniature. The Hawaiian islands are an off-shore suburb of the United States. Only Wake has real time.'

'You were brought up in the Far East?'

'In Manila. My father ran a textile company there.'

'So the Pacific area has a special appeal for you.'

'To some extent. But Wake is a long way from the Philippines.'

Laing never asked if Melville had actually been to Wake Island. Clearly Melville's vision of flying to this remote Pacific atoll was unlikely to take place outside his own head.

However, Melville then had the good luck to discover the aircraft buried in the dunes.

When the tide was in, covering the sand-flats, Melville was forced to walk among the dunes above his beach-house. Driven and shaped by the wind, the contours of the dunes varied from day to day, but one afternoon Melville noticed that a section below the ridge retained its rectilinear form, indicating that some man-made structure lay below the sand, possibly the detached roof of a metal barn or boat-house.

Irritated by the familiar drone of a single-engined aircraft flying from the light airfield behind the resort, Melville clambered up to the ridge through the flowing sand and sat down on the horizontal ledge that ran among the clumps of wild grass. The aircraft, a privately owned Cessna, flew in from the sea directly towards him, banked steeply and circled overhead. Its pilot, a dentist and aviation enthusiast in her early thirties, had been curious about Melville for some time – the mushy drone of her flat six was forever dividing the sky over his head. Often, as he walked across the sand-flats four hundred yards from the shore, she would fly past him, wheels almost touching the streaming sand, throttling up her engine as if trying to din something into his head. She appeared to be testing various types of auxiliary fuel tank. Now and then he saw her driving her American sedan through the deserted streets of the resort towards the airfield. For some reason the noise of her light aircraft began to unsettle him, as if the furniture of his brain was being shifted around behind some dark curtain.

The Cessna circled above him like a dull, unwearying bird. Trying to look as though he was engaged in his study of beach ecology, Melville cleared away the sand between his feet. Without realizing it, he had exposed a section of grey, riveted metal, the skin of an all-too-familiar aerodynamic structure. He stood up and worked away with both hands, soon revealing the unmistakable profile of an aerofoil curvature.

The Cessna had gone, taking the lady dentist back to the air-strip. Melville had forgotten about her as he pushed the heavy sand away, steering it down the saddle between the dunes. Although nearly exhausted, he continued to clear the starboard wing-tip now emerging from the dune. He took off his jacket and beat away the coarse white grains, at last revealing the combat insignia, star and bars of a U.S.A.A.F. roundel.

As he knew within a few minutes, he had discovered an intact wartime B-17. Two days later, by a sustained effort, he had dug away several tons of sand and exposed to view almost the entire starboard wing, the tail and rear turret. The bomber was almost undamaged – Melville assumed that the pilot had run out of fuel while crossing the Channel and tried to land on the sand-flats at low tide, overshot the wet surface and ploughed straight through the dunes above the beach. A write-off, the Fortress had been abandoned where it lay, soon to be covered by the shifting sand-hills. The small resort had been built, flourished briefly and declined without anyone realizing that this relic of World War II lay in the ridge a hundred yards behind the town.

Systematically, Melville organized himself in the task of digging out, and then renovating, this antique bomber. Working by himself, he estimated that it would take three months to expose the aircraft, and a further two years to strip it down and rebuild it from scratch. The precise details of how he would straighten the warped propeller blades and replace the Wright Cyclone engines remained hazy in his mind, but already he visualized the shingle-reinforced earth-and-sand ramp which he would construct with a rented bulldozer from the crest of the dunes down to the beach. When the sea was out, after a long late-summer day, the sand along the tide-line was smooth and hard ...

Few people came to watch him. Tennant, the former advertising man leading the group digging out the Messerschmitt, came across the sand-flats and gazed philosophically at the emerging wings and fuselage of the Fortress. Neither of the men spoke to each other – both, as Melville knew, had something more important on their minds.

In the evening, when Melville was still working on the aircraft, Dr Laing walked along the beach from his solarium. He climbed the shadow-filled dunes, watching Melville clear away the sand from the chin-turret.

'What about the bomb-load?' he asked. 'I'd hate to see the whole town levelled.'

'It's an officially abandoned wreck.' Melville pointed to the stripped-down gun turret. 'Everything has been removed, including the machine-guns and bomb-sight. I think you're safe from me, doctor.'

'A hundred years ago you'd have been digging a

diplodocus out of a chalk cliff,' Laing remarked. The Cessna was circling the sand-bar at the southern end of the resort, returning after a navigation exercise. 'If you're keen to fly perhaps Helen Winthrop will take you on as a co-pilot. She was asking me something about you the other day. She's planning to break the single-engine record to Cape Town.'

This item of news intrigued Melville. The next day, as he worked at his excavation site, he listened for the sound of the Cessna's engine. The image of this determined woman preparing for her solo flight across Africa, testing her aircraft at this abandoned airfield beside the dunes, coincided powerfully with his own dream of flying to Wake Island. He knew full well now that the elderly Fortress he was laboriously digging from the sand-dunes would never leave its perch on the ridge, let alone take off from the beach. But the woman's aircraft offered a feasible alternative. Already he mapped out a route in his mind, calculating the capacity of her auxiliary tanks and the refuelling points in the Azores and Newfoundland.

Afraid that she might leave without him, Melville decided to approach her directly. He drove his car through the deserted streets of the resort, turned on to the unmade road that led to the airfield, and parked beside her American sedan. The Cessna, its engine cowlings removed, stood at the end of the runway.

She was working at an engineering bench in the hangar, welding together the sections of a fuel tank. As Melville approached she switched off the blowtorch and removed her mask, her intelligent face shielded by her hands.

'I see we're involved in a race to get away first,' she called out reassuringly to him when he paused in the entrance to the hangar. 'Dr Laing told me that you'd know how to strengthen these fuel tanks.'

For Melville, her nervous smile cloaked a complex sexual metaphor.

* * *

From the start Melville took it for granted that she would abandon her plan to fly to Cape Town, and instead embark on a round-the-world flight with himself as her co-pilot. He outlined his plans for their westward flight, calculating the reduced fuel load they would carry to compensate for his weight. He showed her his designs for the wing spars and braces that would support the auxiliary tanks.

'Melville, I'm flying to Cape Town,' she told him wearily. 'It's taken me years to arrange this – there's no question of setting out anywhere else. You're obsessed with this absurd island.'

'You'll understand when we get there,' Melville assured her. 'Don't worry about the aircraft. After Wake you'll be on your own. I'll strip off the tanks and cut all these braces away.'

'You intend to stay on Wake Island?' Helen Winthrop seemed unsure of Melville's seriousness, as if listening to an over-enthusiastic patient in her surgery chair outlining the elaborate dental treatment he had set his heart on.

'Stay there? Of course ... ' Melville prowled along the mantelpiece of the beach-house, slapping the line of photographs. 'Look at those runways, everything is there. A big airport like the Wake field is a zone of tremendous possibility – a place of beginnings, by the way, not ends.'

Helen Winthrop made no comment on this, watching Melville quietly. She no longer slept in the hangar at the airstrip, and during her weekend visits moved into Melville's beach-house. Needing his help to increase the Cessna's range, and so reduce the number of refuelling stops with their built-in delays, she put up with his restlessness and child-like excitement, only concerned by his growing dependence on her. As he worked on the Cessna she listened for hours to him describing the runways of the island. However, she was careful never to leave him alone with the ignition keys.

While she was away, working at her dental practice,

Melville returned to the dunes, continuing to dig out the crashed bomber. The port and starboard wings were now free of the sand, soon followed by the upper section of the fuselage. The weekends he devoted to preparing the Cessna for its long westward flight. For all his excitability, the state of controlled euphoria which his soon-to-be-realized dream of flying to Wake Island had brought about, his navigation plans and structural modification to the Cessna's air-frame were carefully and professionally carried through.

Even the intense migraines that began to disturb Melville's sleep did little to dent his good humour. He assumed that these fragments of the past had been brought to the surface of his mind by the strains of his involvement with this over-serious aviatrix, but later he knew that these elements of an unforgotten nightmare had been cued in by the aircraft emerging around him on all sides – Helen Winthrop's Cessna, the Fortress he was exposing to light, the blackened Messerschmitt which the advertising man was lifting from the sea-bed.

After a storm had disturbed the sand-flats, he stood on the balcony of the beach-house inhaling the carbonated air, trying to free himself from the uneasy dreams that had filled the night, a system of demented metaphors. In front of him the surface of the sand-flats was covered with dozens of pieces of rusting metal, aircraft parts shaken loose by the storm. As Helen Winthrop watched from the bedroom window he stepped on to the beach and walked across the ruffled sand, counting the fragments of carburettor and exhaust manifold, trim-tab and tailwheel that lay around him as if left here by the receding tide of his dreams.

Already other memories were massing around him, fragments that he was certain belonged to another man's life, details from the case-history of an imaginary patient whose role he had been tricked into playing. As he worked on the Fortress high among the dunes, brushing the sand away from the cylinder vanes of the radial engines, he remembered other aircraft he had been involved with, vehicles without wings.

The bomber was completely exposed now. Knowing that his work was almost over, Melville opened the ventral crew hatch behind the chin turret. Ever since he had first revealed the cockpit of the plane he had been tempted to climb through the broken starboard windshield and take his seat at the controls, but the experience of the Messerschmitt cautioned him. With Helen Winthrop, however, he would be safe.

Throwing down his spade, he clambered across the sand to the beach-house.

'Helen! Come up here!' He pointed with pride to the exposed aircraft on the ridge, poised on its belly as if at the end of a take-off ramp. While Helen Winthrop tried to calm him, he steered her up the shifting slopes, hand over hand along the rope-line.

As they climbed through the crew hatch he looked back for the last time across the sand-flats, littered with their rusting aircraft parts. Inside the fuselage they searched their way around the barbette of the roof-turret, stepping through the debris of old R/T gear, lifejackets and ammunition boxes. After all his efforts, the interior of the fuselage seemed to Melville like a magical arbour, the grotto-like cavern within some archaic machine.

Sitting beside Helen in the cockpit, happy that she was with him as she would be on their flight across the Pacific, he took her through the controls, moving the throttles and trim wheels.

'Right, now. Mixture rich, carb heat cold, pitch full fine, flaps down for take-off ...'

As she held his shoulders, trying to pull him away from the controls, Melville could hear the engines of the Fortress starting up within his head. As if watching a film, he remembered his years as a military test-pilot, and his single abortive mission as an astronaut. By some grotesque turn of fate, he had become the first astronaut to suffer a mental breakdown in space. His nightmare ramblings had disturbed millions of television viewers around the world, as if the terrifying image of a man going mad in space had triggered off some long-buried innate releasing mechanism.

Later that evening, Melville lay by the window in his bedroom, watching the calm sea that covered the sand-flats. He remembered Helen Winthrop leaving him in the cockpit, and running away along the beach to find Dr Laing. Careful though he was, the physician was no more successful at dealing with Melville than the doctors at the institute of aviation medicine, who had tried to free him from his obsession that he had seen a fourth figure on board the three-man craft. This mysterious figure, either man or bird, he was convinced he had killed. Had he, also, committed the first murder in space? After his release he resolved to make his world-wide journey, externally to Wake Island, and internally across the planets of his mind.

As the summer ended and the time of their departure drew nearer, Melville was forced to renew his efforts at digging out the crashed Fortress. In the cooler weather the night winds moved the sand across the ridge, once again covering the fuselage of the aircraft.

Dr Laing visited him more frequently. Worried by Melville's deteriorating condition, he watched him struggle with the tons of sliding sand.

'Melville, you're exhausting yourself.' Laing took the spade from him and began to shovel away. Melville sat down on the wing. He was careful now never to enter the cockpit. Across the sand-flats Tennant and his team were leaving for the winter, the broken-backed Me 109 carried away on two trucks. Conserving his strength, he waited for the day when he and Helen Winthrop would leave this abandoned resort and take off into the western sky.

'All the radio aids are ready,' he told her on the weekend before they were due to leave. 'All you need to do now is file your flight plan.'

Helen Winthrop watched him sympathetically as he stood by the mantelpiece. Unable to stand his nervous vomiting, she had moved back to the hangar. Despite, or perhaps because of, their brief sexual involvement their relationship now was almost matter-of-factly neutral, but she tried to reassure him.

'How much luggage have you got? You've packed nothing.'

'I'm taking nothing – only the photographs.'

'You won't need them once you get to Wake Island.'

'Perhaps – they're more real for me now than the island could ever be.'

When Helen Winthrop left without him Melville was surprised, but not disappointed. He was working up on the dunes as the heavily laden Cessna, fitted with the wing tanks he had installed, took off from the airstrip. He knew immediately from the pitch of the engine that this was not a trial flight. Sitting on the roof turret of the Fortress, he watched her climb away across the sand-flats, make a steady right-hand turn towards the sea and set off downwind across the Channel.

Long before she was out of sight Melville had forgotten her. He would make his own way to the Pacific. During the following weeks he spent much of his time sheltering under the aircraft, watching the wind blow the sand back across the fuselage. With the departure of Helen Winthrop and the advertising executive with his Messerschmitt he found that his dreams grew calmer, shutting away his memories of the space flights. At times he was certain that his entire memory of having trained as an astronaut was a fantasy, part of some complex delusional system, an extreme metaphor of his real ambition. This conviction brought about a marked improvement in his health and self-confidence.

Even when Dr Laing climbed the dunes and told him that Helen Winthrop had died two weeks after crashing her Cessna at Nairobi airport, Melville had recovered sufficiently to feel several days of true grief. He drove to the airfield and wandered around the empty hangar. Traces of her over-hurried departure, a suitcase of clothes and a spare set of rescue flares, lay among the empty oil-drums.

Returning to the dunes, he continued to dig the crashed bomber from the sand, careful not to expose too much of it to the air. Although often exhausted in the damp winter air, he felt increasingly calm, sustained by the huge bulk of the Fortress, whose cockpit he never entered, and by his dream of flying to Wake Island.

The Life and Death of God

During the spring and summer of 1980 an extraordinary rumour began to sweep the world. At first confined to government and scientific circles in Washington, London and Moscow, it soon spread through Africa, South America and the Far East, and among people in all walks of life, from Australian sheep-farmers to Tokyo night-club hostesses and stockbrokers on the Paris Bourse. Rarely a day passed without the rumour reaching the front pages of at least a dozen newspapers around the world.

In a few countries, notably Canada and Brazil, the persistence of the rumour caused a dangerous drop in commodity prices, and firm denials were issued by the governments of the day. At the United Nations headquarters in New York the Secretary-General appointed a committee of prominent scientists, churchmen and business leaders with the sole purpose of restraining the excitement which the rumour was beginning to generate by the late spring. This, of course, simply convinced everyone that something of universal significance would soon be disclosed.

For once, the governments of the West were helped by the sympathetic attitude of the Soviet Union, and of countries such as Cuba, Libya and North Korea, which in the past would have seized on the smallest advantage the rumour offered them. Yet even this failed to prevent serious outbreaks of industrial unrest and panic-selling – millions of pounds were wiped off the London Stock Exchange after the announcement that the Archbishop of Canterbury would visit the Holy Land. A plague of absenteeism swept across the world in the rumour's wake. In areas as far apart as the automotive plants of Detroit and the steel foundries of the Ruhr, entire working populations lost all interest in their jobs and sauntered through the factory gates, gazing amiably at the open sky.

Fortunately, the rumour's effects were generally pacific and non-violent. In the Middle East and Asia, where it confirmed beliefs already held for centuries, the news raised barely a ripple of interest, and only in the most sophisticated government and scientific circles was there anything of a flurry. Without doubt, the impact of the rumour was greatest in Western Europe and North America. Ironically, it was most rife in those two countries, the United States and Britain, which for centuries had claimed to base their entire societies on the ideals expressed by it.

During this period one body alone kept aloof from all this speculation—the world's churches and religious faiths. This is not to say that they were in any way hostile or indifferent, but their attitude indicated a certain wariness, if not a distinct ambivalence. Although they could hardly deny the rumour, priests and clergymen everywhere recommended a due caution in the minds of their congregations, a reluctance to jump too eagerly to conclusions.

However, a remarkable and unexpected development soon took place. In a solemn declaration, representatives of the world's great religious faiths, meeting simultaneously in Rome, Mecca and Jerusalem, stated that they had at last decided to abandon their rivalries and differences. Together they would now join hands in a new and greater church, to be called the United Faith Assembly, international and interdenominational in character, which would contain the essential elements of all creeds in a single unified faith.

The news of this extraordinary development at last forced the governments of the world to a decision. On

August 28th a plenary meeting of the United Nations was held. In a fanfare of publicity that exceeded anything known even by that organization, there was an unprecedented attendance from delegates of every member nation. As the commentators of a hundred television channels carried descriptions of the scene all over the world, a great concourse of scientists, statesmen and scholars, preceded by representatives of the United Faith Assembly, entered the United Nations building and took their seats.

When the meeting began the President of the United Nations called on a succession of prominent scientists, led by the director of the radio-observatory at Jodrell Bank in Britain. After a preamble in which he recalled science's quest for the unifying principle that lay behind the apparent uncertainty and caprice of nature, he described the remarkable research work undertaken during recent years with the telescopes at Jodrell Bank and Arecibo in Puerto Rico. Just as the discovery of radioactivity had stemmed from the realization that even smaller particles existed within the apparently indivisible atom, so these two giant telescopes had revealed that all electromagnetic radiations in fact contained a system of infinitely smaller vibrations. These 'ultra-microwaves', as they had been called, permeated all matter and space.

However, the speaker continued, a second and vastly more important discovery had been made when the structure of these microwaves was analysed by computer. This almost intangible electromagnetic system unmistakably exhibited a complex and continuously changing mathematical structure with all the attributes of intelligence. To give only one example, it responded to the behaviour of the human observer and was even sensitive to his unspoken thoughts. Exhaustive studies of the phenomenon confirmed beyond all doubt that this sentient being, as it must be called, pervaded the entire universe. More exactly, it provided the basic substratum of which the universe was composed. The very air they were breathing in the assembly hall at that moment, their minds and bodies, were formed by this intelligent being of infinite dimensions.

At the conclusion of the statement a profound silence spread through the General Assembly, and from there to the world beyond. In cities and towns all over the earth the streets were deserted, traffic abandoned as people waited quietly by their television sets. The President of the United Nations then rose and read out a declaration signed by three hundred scientists and divines. After two years of the most rigorous tests the existence of a supreme deity had been proved beyond a shadow of doubt. Mankind's age-old faith in a divine principle had at last been scientifically confirmed, and a new epoch in human history would unfold before them.

The next day the newspapers of the world bore a hundred variants of the same headline:

GOD EXISTS

Supreme Being Pervades Universe

During the following weeks the events of ordinary life were forgotten. All over the world services of thanksgiving were held, religious processions filled countless streets. Vast gatherings of penitents thronged the sacred cities and shrines of the world. Moscow, New York, Tokyo and London resembled medieval towns on an apocalyptic saint's day. Heads raised to the skies, millions knelt in the streets, or walked in slow cavalcades, crosses and mandalas held before them. The cathedrals of St Peter's, Notre Dame and St Patrick's were forced to hold continuous services, so great were the crowds that flocked through their doors. Sectarian feuds were forgotten. Priests of the United Faith Assembly exchanged vestments and officiated at each other's services. Buddhists were baptized, Christians turned prayer-wheels and Jews knelt before the statues of Krishna and Zoroaster.

More practical benefits were to follow. Everywhere doctors reported a marked drop in the numbers of their patients. Neuroses and other mental ills disappeared overnight, as the discovery of the deity's existence worked its instant therapy. All over the world police-forces were disbanded. Members of the armed services were sent on indefinite leave pending demobilization, long-closed frontiers were unsealed. The Berlin Wall was dismantled. Everywhere people behaved as if some immense victory had been won against an invincible enemy. Here and there, between particularly aggressive rivals, such as the United States and Cuba, Egypt and Israel, long-standing pacts of friendship were signed. Military aircraft and naval fleets were sent to the scrapyards, stockpiles of weapons were destroyed. (However, a few sporting rifles were retained when the spirit of universal brotherhood produced its first casualty – a Swedish engineer in Bengal who attempted to embrace a tiger. Warnings were issued that an awareness of God's existence had yet to extend to the lower members of the animal kingdom, where for the time being the struggle for life remained as pitiless as ever.)

To begin with, such isolated episodes were barely noticed in the general euphoria. Thousands of spectators sat around the great telescopes at Jodrell Bank and Arecibo, not to mention a number of commercial TV aerials and any other structures that vaguely resembled radio antennae, waiting patiently for a direct message from the Almighty. Gradually people drifted back to work – or, more exactly, those returned who considered their work morally gainful. Manufacturing industry was able to keep going, but the agencies responsible for selling its products to the public found themselves in a dilemma. The elements of guile and exaggeration at the basis of all merchandizing, whether on the level of nationwide advertising campaigns or door-to-door salesmanship, were no longer tolerable under the new dispensation, but no alternative machinery of distribution was available.

The inevitable slackening of commerce and industry seemed unimportant during these first weeks. The majority of people in Europe and the United States were still celebrating a new estate of man, the beginnings of the first true millennium. The whole basis of private life had changed, and with it attitudes towards sex, morality and all human relationships. Newspapers and television had been transformed – the previous diet of crime reports and political gossip, westerns and soap-operas had given way to serious articles and programmes elaborating the background to the discovery of the deity.

This growing interest in the precise nature of the godhead led to a closer examination of its presumed moral nature. Despite the generalizations of scientists and clergy, it was soon clear that the dimensions of the supreme being were large enough to embrace any interpretation one cared to invent. Although the deity's overall moral purpose could be assumed from the harmony, purity and formal symmetry that the mathematical analyses revealed – qualities more pronounced in response to cohesive and creative actions than to random or destructive ones – these characteristics seemed little more specific in relation to man and his day-to-day behaviour than the principles underlying music. Without doubt a supreme intelligence existed whose being permeated the entire fabric of the universe, flowing in a myriad ripples through their minds and bodies like an infinite moral ether, but this deity seemed far less ready with explicit demands and directives than it had been in its previous incarnations.

Fortunately, their god was clearly neither a jealous nor a vengeful one. No thunderbolt fell from the sky. The first fears of a judgment day, of darkening landscapes covered with gibbets, safely receded. The nightmares of Bosch and Breughel failed to materialize. And for once humanity needed no goads to make it regulate its conduct. Marital infidelities, promiscuity and divorce had almost vanished.

Curiously, there was also a drop in the number of marriages, perhaps because of a common feeling that some sort of a millennial kingdom was at hand.

This widespread notion revealed itself in many ways. Great numbers of industrial workers in Europe and North America had lost all interest in their jobs, and sat about on their doorsteps with their neighbours, gazing at the sky and listening to the radio bulletins. At the summer's end farmers harvested their crops but seemed much less enthusiastic about preparing for the coming season. The flow of pronouncements, and the first disputed interpretations, from the committees of divines and scientists still investigating the phenomenon of the deity suggested that it might be unwise to plan too carefully on an indefinite future.

Within two months of the confirmation of the world-wide rumour of God's existence came the first indications of government concern over the consequences. Industry and agriculture were already affected, though far less than commerce, politics and advertising. Everywhere the results of this new sense of morality, of the virtues of truth and charity, were becoming clear. A legion of overseers, time-keepers and inspectors found themselves no longer needed. Long-established advertising agencies became bankrupt. Accepting the public demand for total honesty, and fearful of that supreme client up in the sky, the majority of television commercials now ended with an exhortation *not* to buy their products.

As for the world of politics, its whole *raison d'être*—its appeals to self-assertion, intrigue and nepotism—had been destroyed. A dozen parliaments, from the U.S. Congress to the Russian Chamber of Deputies and the British House of Commons, found themselves deprived of the very machinery of their existence.

The United Faith Assembly was faced with equal problems. Although people still attended their places of worship in larger numbers than ever before, they were doing so at times other than those of the formal services, communuing directly with the Almighty rather than playing the part of a subordinate laity in a ritual mediated to them through a priesthood.

The former Christian members of the United Faith Assembly, who remembered the Reformation and Martin Luther's revolt against a clergy claiming privileged access to the supreme being, were of course perturbed by these developments. They were reluctant to accept the mathematical description of the deity offered by the world's scientists, but had nothing to offer in its place and for the time being were on the defensive. The physicists, conversely, were only too quick to remind the clergy that their long-hallowed symbols–cross, trinity and mandala–were based more on fancy than on the scientific reality which they themselves had made available. The long-standing fear of all churches, that the revelation of God might come from knowledge rather than faith, had at last been justified.

The continued change in the character of life on both sides of the Atlantic began to disturb prominent members of government and industry. Conditions in the United States and Northern Europe were beginning to resemble those in India and the Far East, where legions of amiable beggars wandered the streets without a thought for the morrow. The Kingdom of God might be at hand, but that hand was empty.

During October little happened on the surface of events, but at the end of the month a second meeting of the United Faith Assembly was held in Jerusalem. Here a prominent archbishop publicly challenged the scientific view of the deity as a being of vast neutral intelligence. Without doubt, the archbishop affirmed, this was to take a naive and over-simplified view based on what were admitted to be crude methods of detection. Was the deity entirely passive or, like the sea, did it reveal itself in many forms and moods? Remarking that he was not ashamed to refer to the Manichean Heresy, the archbishop stressed the dualism of good and evil that had always existed in the past, in man as in nature, and which would continue to exist in the future. This was not to suggest that evil was a fundamental part of man's nature, or that he was incapable of redemption, but this passive contemplation of an invisible God should not be allowed to blind them to the inevitable antagonisms within themselves, or indeed to their own failings. The great achievements of mankind, its commerce, art and industry, had been based on this sound understanding of the dual nature of mankind and its motives. The present decline of civilized life was a symptom of the refusal to see themselves as they were, a warning of the dangers of identifying themselves too closely with the Almighty. The capacity for sin was a prerequisite of redemption.

Soon afterwards, as if cued in by the archbishop, a series of spectacular crimes took place around the world. In the Middle West of the United States a number of bank robberies were carried out which rivalled those of the 1930s. In London there was an armed assault on the crown jewels in the Tower. A host of minor larcenies followed. Not all these crimes were committed for reasons of gain. In Paris the Mona Lisa was slashed by a maniac running amok in the Louvre, while in Cologne the high altar of the Cathedral was desecrated by vandals apparently protesting against the very existence of the deity.

The attitude of the United Faith Assembly to these crimes was unexpected. It greeted them with patient tolerance, as if relieved to see these familiar examples of human frailty. After the arrest of a noted wife-poisoner in Alsace a local priest pronounced that the man's guilt was in fact a testimony to his innocence, a sign of his capacity for eventual redemption.

This tortuous paradox was to receive a great deal of publicity. A number of less scrupulous politicians began to foment similar notions. One Congressional candidate, in a badly hit area of California where military aircraft had been manufactured, suggested that the notion of an all-pervading deity was an affront to the free choice and diversity of human activity. The sense of a closed world reduced man's powers of initiative and self-reliance, the qualities on which the free-enterprise democracies had built their greatness.

This statement was soon followed by the speech of a distinguished metaphysician attending a congress in Zürich. He referred to the plurality of the universe, to its infinite phenomenology. To embrace all possibilities the deity would have to contain the possibility of its own non-being. In other words, it belonged to that class of open-ended structures whose form, extent and identity were impossible to define. The term 'deity' was, in any useful sense, meaningless.

The scientists at Jodrell Bank and Arecibo who had first identified the Almighty were asked to reconsider their original findings. The televised hearings in Washington, at which the tired-eyed astro-physicists were harassed and cross-examined by teams of lawyers and divines, recalled a latter-day Inquisition. At Jodrell Bank and Arecibo troops were called in to protect the telescopes from crowds of over-hasty converts.

The fierce debates which followed were watched with great attention by the public. By now, in early December, the Christmas season was getting under way, but without any of its usual enthusiasm. For one thing, few stores and shops had anything for sale. In addition, there was little money to spare. The rationing of some basic commodities had been introduced. In many ways life was becoming intolerable. Hotels and restaurants were without service. Cars were forever breaking down.

Everywhere, as the debate continued, people turned to the United Faith Assembly. Mysteriously, however, almost all churches were closed, mosques and synagogues, shrines and temples remained sealed to the unsettled crowds. Members of congregations were now selected as strictly as those of the most exclusive clubs, and applicants were admitted only if they agreed to accept the church's guidance on all spiritual matters, its absolute authority in all religious affairs. A rumour began that an announcement of world-wide importance would shortly be made, but that this time it would be given only to the faithful.

The mounting atmosphere of unease and uncertainty was distracted for a few days by the news of several natural disasters. A landslip in northern Peru immolated a thousand villagers. In Yugoslavia an earthquake shattered a provincial capital. Icebergs sank a supertanker in the Atlantic. The question asked tentatively by a New York newspaper,

DOES GOD EXIST?
Faith Assembly casts doubt on Deity

was relegated to a back page.

Three weeks before Christmas, war broke out between Israel and Egypt. The Chinese invaded Nepal, reclaiming territory which they had only recently ceded while under the spell of what they termed a 'neo-colonialist' machination. A week later revolution in Italy, backed by the church and military, ousted the previous liberal régime. Industrial output began to revive in the United States and Europe. Russian missile-firing submarines were detected on manoeuvres in the North Atlantic. On Christmas Eve the world's seismographs recorded a gigantic explosion in the area of the Gobi Desert, and Peking Radio announced the successful testing of a 100-megaton hydrogen bomb. Christmas decorations had at last appeared in the streets, the familiar figures of Santa Claus and his reindeer hung over a thousand department-stores. Carol festivals were held before open congregations in a hundred cathedrals.

In all this festivity few people heeded the publication

of what was described by a spokesman of the United Faith Assembly as one of the most far-reaching and revolutionary religious statements ever made, the Christmas encyclical entitled *God is Dead* ...

The Greatest Television Show on Earth

The discovery in the year 2001 of an effective system of time travel had a number of important repercussions, nowhere greater than in the field of television. The last quarter of the twentieth century had seen the spectacular growth of television across every continent on the globe, and the programmes transmitted by the huge American, European and Afro-Asian networks each claimed audiences of a billion viewers. Yet despite their enormous financial resources the television companies were faced with a chronic shortage of news and entertainment. Vietnam, the first TV War, had given viewers all the excitement of live transmissions from the battlefield, but wars in general, not to mention newsworthy activity of any kind, had died out as the world's population devoted itself almost exclusively to watching television.

At this point the discovery of time travel made its fortunate appearance.

As soon as the first spate of patent suits had been settled (one Japanese entrepreneur almost succeeded in copyrighting history; time was then declared 'open' territory) it became clear that the greatest obstacle to time travel was not the laws of the physical universe but the vast sums of money needed to build and power the installations. These safaris into the past cost approximately a million dollars a minute. After a few brief journeys to verify the Crucifixion, the signing of Magna Carta and Columbus's discovery of the Americas, the government-financed Einstein Memorial Time Centre at Princeton was forced to suspend operations.

Plainly, only one other group could finance further

explorations into the past – the world's television corporations. Their eager assurances that there would be no undue sensationalism convinced government leaders that the educational benefits of these travelogues through time outweighed any possible lapses in taste.

The television companies, for their part, saw in the past an inexhaustible supply of first-class news and entertainment – all of it, moreover, free. Immediately they set to work, investing billions of dollars, rupees, roubles and yen in duplicating the great chronotron at the Princeton Time Centre. Task-forces of physicists and mathematicians were enrolled as assistant producers. Camera crews were sent to key sites – London, Washington and Peking – and shortly afterwards the first pilot programmes were transmitted to an eager world.

These blurry scenes, like faded newsreels, of the coronation of Queen Elizabeth II, the inauguration of Franklin Delano Roosevelt and the funeral of Mao Tse-tung triumphantly demonstrated the feasibility of Time Vision. After this solemn unveiling – a gesture in the direction of the government watchdog committees – the television companies began seriously to plan their schedules. The winter programmes for the year 2002 offered viewers the assassination of President Kennedy ('live', as the North American company tactlessly put it), the D-Day landings and the Battle of Stalingrad. Asian viewers were given Pearl Harbour and the fall of Corregidor.

This emphasis on death and destruction set the pace for what followed. The success of the programmes was beyond the planners' wildest dreams. These fleeting glimpses of smoke-crossed battlegrounds, with their burnt-out tanks and landing craft, had whetted an enormous appetite. More and more camera crews were readied, and an army of military historians deployed to establish the exact time at which Bastogne was relieved, the victory flags hoisted above Mount Suribachi and the Reichstag.

Within a year a dozen programmes each week brought

to three billion viewers the highlights of World War II and the subsequent decades, all transmitted as they actually occurred. Night after night, somewhere around the world, John F. Kennedy was shot dead in Dealey Plaza, atom bombs exploded over Hiroshima and Nagasaki, Adolf Hitler committed suicide in the ruins of his Berlin bunker.

After this success the television companies moved back to the 1914–18 War, ready to reap an even richer harvest of audience ratings from the killing grounds of Passchendaele and Verdun. To their surprise, however, the glimpses of this mud- and shell-filled universe were a dismal failure compared with the great technological battles of World War II being transmitted live at the same time on rival channels from the carrier decks of the Philippine Sea and the thousand-bomber raids over Essen and Dusseldorf.

One sequence alone from World War I quickened the viewers' jaded palates – a cavalry charge by Uhlans of the German Imperial Army. Riding over the barbed wire on their splendid mounts, white plumes flying above the mud, these lance-wielding horsemen brought to a billion war-weary TV screens the magic of pageantry and costume. At a moment when it might have faltered, Time Vision was saved by the epaulette and the cuirass.

Immediately, camera crews began to travel back into the nineteenth century. World Wars I and II faded from the screen. Within a few months viewers saw the coronation of Queen Victoria, the assassination of Lincoln and the siege of the Alamo.

As a climax to this season of instant history, the great Time Vision corporations of Europe and North America collaborated on their most spectacular broadcast to date – a live coverage of the defeat of Napoleon Bonaparte at the Battle of Waterloo.

While making their preparations the two companies made

a discovery that was to have far-reaching consequences for the whole history of Time Vision. During their visits to the battle (insulated from the shot and fury by the invisible walls of their time capsules) the producers found that there were fewer combatants actually present than described by the historians of the day. Whatever the immense political consequences of the defeat of Napoleonic France, the battle itself was a disappointing affair, a few thousand march-wearied troops engaged in sporadic rifle and artillery duels.

An emergency conference of programme chiefs discussed this failure of Waterloo to live up to its reputation. Senior producers revisited the battlefield, leaving their capsules to wander in disguise among the exhausted soldiery. The prospect of the lowest audience ratings in the history of Time Vision seemed hourly more imminent.

At this crisis-point some nameless assistant producer came up with a remarkable idea. Rather than sit back helplessly behind their cameras, the Time Vision companies should step in themselves, he suggested, lending their vast expertise and resources to heightening the drama of the battle. More extras – that is, mercenaries recruited from the nearby farming communities – could be thrown into the fray, supplies of powder and shot distributed to the empty guns, and the entire choreography of the battle re-vamped by the military consultants in the editorial departments. 'History', he concluded, 'is just a first draft screenplay.'

This suggestion of re-making history to boost its audience appeal was seized upon. Equipped with a lavish supply of gold coinage, agents of the television companies moved across the Belgian and North German plains, hiring thousands of mercenaries (at the standard rate for TV extras of fifty dollars per day on location, regardless of rank, seventy-five dollars for a speaking part). The relief column of the Prussian General Blücher, reputed by historians to be many thousand strong and to have decisively turned the battle against Napoleon, was in fact found to be a puny force of brigade strength. Within a few days thousands of eager recruits flocked to the colours, antibiotics secretly administered to polluted water supplies cured a squadron of cavalry hunters suffering from anthrax, and a complete artillery brigade threatened with typhus was put on its feet by a massive dose of chloromycetin.

The Battle of Waterloo, when finally transmitted to an audience of over one billion viewers, was a brilliant spectacle more than equal to its advance publicity of the past two hundred years. The thousands of mercenaries fought with savage fury, the air was split by non-stop artillery barrages, waves of cavalry charged and recharged. Napoleon himself was completely bewildered by the way events turned out, spending his last years in baffled exile.

After the success of Waterloo the Time Vision companies realized the advantages of preparing their ground. From then onwards almost all important historical events were rescripted by the editorial departments. Hannibal's army crossing the Alps was found to contain a mere half-dozen elephants — two hundred more were provided to trample down the dumbfounded Romans. Caesar's assassins numbered only two – five additional conspirators were hired. Famous historical orations, such as the Gettysburg Address, were cut and edited to make them more stirring. Waterloo, meanwhile, was not forgotten. To recoup the original investment the battle was sublet to smaller TV contractors, some of whom boosted the battle to a scale resembling Armageddon. However, these spectacles in the De Mille manner, in which rival companies appeared on the same battlefield, pouring in extras, weapons and animals, were looked down on by more sophisticated viewers.

To the annoyance of the television companies, the most fascinating subject in the whole of history remained barred to them. At the stern insistence of the Christian churches the entire events surrounding the life of Christ were kept off the screen. Whatever the spiritual benefits of hearing the Sermon on the Mount transmitted live might be, these were tempered by the prospect of this sublime experience being faded out between beatitudes for the commercial breaks.

Baulked here, the programmers moved further back in time. To celebrate the fifth anniversary of Time Vision, preparations began for a stupendous joint venture – the flight of the Israelites from Egypt and the crossing of the Red Sea. A hundred camera units and several thousand producers and technicians took up their positions in the Sinai Peninsula. Two months before the transmission it was obvious that there would now be more than two sides in this classic confrontation between the armies of Egypt and the children of the Lord. Not only did the camera crews outnumber the forces of either side, but the hiring of Egyptian extras, additional wave-making equipment and the prefabricated barrage built to support the cameras might well prevent the Israelites from getting across at all. Clearly, the powers of the Almighty would be severely tested in his first important confrontation with the ratings.

A few forebodings were expressed by the more old-fashioned clerics, printed under ironic headlines such as 'War against Heaven?', 'Sinai Truce Offer rejected by TV Producers Guild'. At bookmakers throughout Europe and the United States the odds lengthened against the Israelites. On the day of transmission, January 1st, 2006, the audience ratings showed that 98% of the Western world's adult viewers were by their sets.

The first pictures appeared on the screens. Under a fitful sky the fleeing Israelites plodded into view, advancing towards the invisible cameras mounted over the water. Originally three hundred in number, the Israelites now formed a vast throng that stretched with its baggage train for several miles across the desert. Confused by the great press of camp-followers, the Israelite leaders paused on the shore, uncertain how to cross this shifting mass of unstable water. Along the horizon the sabre-wheeled chariots of Pharaoh's army raced towards them.

The viewers watched spellbound, many wondering whether the television companies had at last gone too far.

Then, without explanation, a thousand million screens went blank.

Pandemonium broke loose. Everywhere switchboards were jammed. Priority calls at inter-governmental level jammed the Comsat relays, the Time Vision studios in Europe and America were besieged.

Nothing came through. All contacts with the camera crews on location had been broken. Finally, two hours later, a brief picture appeared, of racing waters swilling over the shattered remains of television cameras and switchgear. On the near bank, the Egyptian forces turned for home. Across the waters, the small band of Israelites moved towards the safety of Sinai.

What most surprised the viewers was the eerie light that illuminated the picture, as if some archaic but extraordinary method of power were being used to transmit it.

No further attempts to regain contact succeeded. Almost all the world's Time Vision equipment had been destroyed, its leading producers and technicians lost for ever, perhaps wandering the stony rocks of Sinai like a second lost tribe. Shortly after this débâcle, these safaris into the past were eliminated from the world's TV programmes. As one priest with a taste for ironic humour remarked to his chastened television congregation: 'The big channel up in the sky has its ratings too.'

A Place and a Time to Die

Shotguns levelled, the two men waited on the river bank. From the shore facing them, four hundred yards across the bright spring water, the beating of gongs and drums sounded through the empty air, echoing off the metal roofs of the abandoned town. Fire-crackers burst over the trees along the shore, the mushy pink explosions lighting up the gun-barrels of tanks and armoured cars.

All morning the ill-matched couple making this last stand together – Mannock, the retired and now slightly eccentric police chief, and his reluctant deputy, Forbis, a thyroidal used-car salesman – had watched the mounting activity on the opposite shore. Soon after eight o'clock when Mannock drove through the deserted town, the first arrivals had already appeared on the scene. Four scout-cars carrying a platoon of soldiers in padded brown uniforms were parked on the bank. The officer scanned Mannock through his binoculars for a few seconds and then began to inspect the town. An hour later an advance battalion of field engineers took up their position by the dynamited railroad bridge. By noon an entire division had arrived. A dusty caravan of self-propelled guns, tanks on trailers, and mobile field-kitchens in commandeered buses rolled across the farmland and pulled to a halt by the bank. After them came an army of infantry and camp-followers, pulling wooden carts and beating gongs.

Earlier that morning Mannock had climbed the water-tower at his brother's farm. The landscape below the mountains ten miles away was criss-crossed with dozens of motorized columns. Most of them were moving in an apparently random way, half the time blinded by their own dust. Like an advancing horde of ants, they spilled across the abandoned farmland, completely ignoring an intact town and then homing on an empty grain silo.

By now, though, in the early afternoon, all sections of this huge field army had reached the river. Any hopes Mannock had kept alive that they might turn and disappear towards the horizon finally faded. When exactly they would choose to make their crossing was hard to gauge. As he and Forbis watched, a series of enormous camps was being set up. Lines of collapsible huts marked out barrack squares, squads of soldiers marched up and down in the dust, rival groups of civilians – presumably political cadres – drilled and shouted slogans. The smoke from hundreds of mess fires rose into the air, blocking off Mannock's view of the blue-chipped mountains that had formed the backdrop to the river valley during the twenty years he had spent there. Rows of camouflaged trucks and amphibious vehicles waited along the shore, but there was still no sign of any crossing. Tank-crews wandered about like bored gangs on a boardwalk, letting off fire-crackers and flying paper kites with slogans painted on their tails. Everywhere the beating of gongs and drums went on without pause.

'There must be a million of them there – for God's sake, they'll never get over!' Almost disappointed, Forbis lowered his shotgun on to the sandbag emplacement.

'Nothing's stopped them yet,' Mannock commented. He pointed to a convoy of trucks dragging a flotilla of wooden landing-craft across a crowded parade ground. 'Sampans – they look crazy, don't they?'

While Forbis glared across the river Mannock looked down at him, with difficulty controlling the distaste he felt whenever he realized exactly whom he had chosen as his last companion. A thin, bitter-mouthed man with over-large eyes, Forbis was one of that small group of people Mannock had instinctively disliked throughout his entire life. The past few days in the empty town had confirmed all his prejudices. The previous afternoon, after an hour spent driving around the town and shooting at the stray dogs, Forbis had taken Mannock back to his house. There he had proudly shown off his huge home arsenal. Bored by this display of weapons, Mannock wandered into the dining-room, only to find the table laid out like an altar with dozens of far-right magazines, pathological hate-sheets and heaven knew what other nonsense printed on crude home presses.

What had made Forbis stay behind in the deserted town after everyone else had gone? What made him want to defend these few streets where he had never been particularly liked or successful? Some wild gene or strange streak of patriotism – perhaps not all that far removed from his own brand of cantankerousness. Mannock looked across the water as a huge catherine-wheel revolved into the air above a line of tanks parked along the shore, its puffy pink smoke turning the encampment into an enormous carnival. For a moment a surge of hope went through Mannock that this vast army might be driven by wholly peaceful motives, that it might suddenly decide to withdraw, load its tanks on to their trailers and move off to the western horizon.

As the light faded he knew all too well that there was no chance of this happening. Generations of hate and resentment had driven these people in their unbroken advance across the world, and here in this town in a river valley they would take a small part of their revenge.

Why had he himself decided to stay behind, waiting here behind these few useless sandbags with a shotgun in his hands? Mannock glanced back at the water-tower that marked the north-west perimeter of his brother's farm, for years the chief landmark of the town. Until the last moment he had planned to leave with the rest of the family, helping to gas up the cars and turn loose what was left of the livestock. Closing his own house down for the last time, he decided to wait until the dust subsided when the great exodus began. He drove down to the river, and stood under the broken span of the bridge which the army engineers had dynamited before they retreated.

Walking southwards along the shore, he had nearly been shot by Forbis. The salesman had dug himself into a homemade roadblock above the bank, and was waiting there all alone for his first sight of the enemy. Mannock tried to persuade him to leave with the others, but as he remonstrated with Forbis he realized that he was talking to himself, and why he sounded so unconvincing.

For the next days, as the distant dust-clouds moved towards them from the horizon, turning the small valley into an apocalyptic landscape, the two men formed an uneasy alliance. Forbis looked on impatiently as Mannock moved through the empty streets, closing the doors of the abandoned cars and parking them along the kerb, shutting the windows of the houses and putting lids on the garbage pails. With his crazy logic Forbis really believed that the two of them could hold up the advance of this immense army.

'Maybe for only a few hours,' he assured Mannock with quiet pride. 'But that'll be enough.'

A few seconds, more likely, Mannock reflected. There would be a brief bloody flurry somewhere, one burst from a machine-pistol and quietus in the dust ...

'Mannock—!' Forbis pointed to the shore fifty yards from the bridge embankment. A heavy metal skiff was being manhandled into the water by a labour-platoon. A tank backed along the shore behind it, test-rotating its turret. Exhaust belched from its diesel.

'They're coming!' Forbis crouched behind the sandbags, levelling his shotgun. He beckoned furiously at Mannock. 'For God's sake, Mannock, get your head down!'

Mannock ignored him. He stood on the roof of the emplacement, his figure fully exposed. He watched the skiff slide into the water. While two of the crew tried to start the motor, a squad in the bows rowed it across to the first bridge pylon. No other craft were being launched, In fact, as Mannock had noted already, no one was looking across the river at all, though any good marksman could have hit them both without difficulty. A single 75mm. shell from one of the tanks would have disposed of them and the emplacement.

'Engineers,' he told Forbis. 'They're checking the bridge supports. Maybe they want to rebuild it first.'

Forbis peered doubtfully through his binoculars, then relaxed his grip on the shotgun. His jaw was still sticking forward aggressively. Watching him, Mannock realized that Forbis genuinely wasn't afraid of what would happen to them. He glanced back at the town. There was a flash of light as an upstairs door turned and caught the sun.

'Where are you going?' A look of suspicion was on Forbis's face, reinforcing the doubts he already felt about Mannock. 'They may come sooner than you think.'

'They'll come in their own time, not ours,' Mannock said. 'Right now it looks as if even they don't know. I'll be here.'

He walked stiffly towards his car, conscious of the target his black leather jacket made against the white station-wagon. At any moment the bright paintwork could be shattered by a bullet carrying pieces of his heart.

He started the motor and reversed carefully on to the beach. Through the rear-view mirror he watched the opposite shore. The engineers in the skiff had lost interest in the bridge. Like a party of sight-seers they drifted along the shore, gazing up at the tank-crews squatting on their turrets. The noise of gongs beat across the water.

In the deserted town the sounds murmured in the metal roofs. Mannock drove round the railroad station and the bus depot, checking if any refugees had arrived after crossing the river. Nothing moved. Abandoned cars filled the side-streets. Broken store windows formed jagged frames around piles of detergent packs and soup cans. In the filling stations the slashed pump hoses leaked their last gasolene across the unwashed concrete.

Mannock stopped the car in the centre of the town. He stepped out and looked up at the windows of the hotel and the public library. By some acoustic freak the noise of the gongs had faded, and for a moment it seemed like any drowsy afternoon ten years earlier.

Mannock leaned into the back seat of the car and took out a paper parcel. Fumbling with the dry string, he finally unpicked the ancient knot, then unwrapped the paper and took out a faded uniform jacket.

Searching for a cigarette pack in his hip pockets, Mannock examined the worn braid. He had planned this small gesture – a pointless piece of sentimentality, he well knew – as a private goodbye to himself and the town, but the faded metal badges had about the same relevance to reality as the rusty hubcap lying in the gutter a few feet away. Tossing it over his left arm, he opened the door of the car.

Before he could drop the jacket on to the seat a rifle shot slammed across the square. A volley of echoes boomed off the buildings. Mannock dropped to one knee behind the car, his head lowered from the third-floor windows of the hotel. The bullet had starred the passenger window and richocheted off the dashboard, chipping the steering wheel before exiting through the driver's door.

As the sounds of the explosion faded, Mannock could hear the rubber boots of a slimly built man moving down the fire-escape behind the building. Mannock looked upwards. High above the town a strange flag flew from the mast of the hotel. So the first snipers had moved in across the river. His blood quickening, Mannock drew his shotgun from the seat of the car.

Some five minutes later he was waiting in the alley

behind the supermarket when a running figure darted past him. As the man crashed to the gravel Mannock straddled him with both legs, the shotgun levelled at his face. Mannock looked down, expecting to find a startled yellow-skinned youth in quilted uniform.

'Forbis?'

The salesman clambered to his knees, painfully catching back his breath. He stared at the blood on his hands, and then at Mannock's face above the barrel of the shotgun.

'What the *hell* are you playing at?' he gasped in a weary voice, one ear cocked for any sounds from the river. 'That shot – do you want to bring them over?' He gestured at the police jacket which Mannock was now wearing, and then shook his head sadly. 'Mannock, this isn't a fancy-dress party ... '

Mannock was about to explain to him when a car door slammed. The engine of the station-wagon roared above the squeal of tyres. As the two men reached the sidewalk the car was swerving out of the square, bumper knocking aside a pile of cartons.

'Hathaway!' Forbis shouted. 'Did you see him? There's your sniper, Mannock!'

Mannock watched the car plunge out of sight down a side-street. 'Hathaway,' he repeated dourly. 'I should have guessed. He's decided to stay and meet his friends.'

After Forbis had torn the flag down from the hotel mast he and Mannock drove back to the river. Mannock sat uncomfortably in the police jacket, thinking of Hathaway, that strange youth who with himself and Forbis completed one key triangle within their society: Hathaway the misfit, head full of half-baked Marxist slogans, saddled with a bored wife who one day tired of living in rooming-houses and walked out on him, taking their small son; Hathaway the failed political activist, whose obsessed eyes were too much even for a far-left student group; Hathaway the petty criminal, arrested for pilfering a supermarket—though he soon convinced himself that he was a martyr to the capitalist conspiracy.

No doubt one sight of Mannock's old police jacket had been enough.

An hour later the advance began across the river. One minute Mannock was sitting on the old rail-tie that formed the rear wall of Forbis's emplacement, watching the endless parades and drilling that were taking place on the opposite shore, and listening to the gongs and exploding fire-crackers. The next minute dozens of landing-craft were moving down the bank into the water. Thousands of soldiers swarmed after them, bales of equipment held over their heads. The whole landscape had risen up and heaved forward. Half a mile inland vast dust-clouds were climbing into the air. Everywhere the collapsible huts and command posts were coming down, ungainly cranes swung pontoon sections over the trees. The beating of drums sounded for miles along the water's edge. Counting quickly, Mannock estimated that at least fifty landing-craft were crossing the water, each towing two or three amphibious tanks behind it.

One large wooden landing-craft was headed straight towards them, well over a hundred infantrymen squatting on the deck like coolies. Above the square teak bows a heavy machine-gun jutted through its rectangular metal shield, the gunners signalling to the helmsman.

As Forbis fumbled with his shotgun Mannock knocked the butt off his shoulder.

'Fall back! Nearer the town—they'll come right over us here!'

Crouching down, they backed away from the emplacement. As the first landing-craft hit the shore they reached the cover of the trees lining the road. Forbis sprinted ahead to a pile of fifty-gallon drums lying in the ditch and began to roll them around into a crude emplacement.

Mannock watched him working away, as the air was

filled with the noise of tank-engines and gongs. When Forbis had finished Mannock shook his head. He pointed with a tired hand at the fields on either side of the road, then leaned his shotgun against the wall of the ditch.

As far as they could see, hundreds of soldiers were moving up towards the town, rifles and submachine-guns slung over their shoulders. The river bank was crammed with landing-craft. A dozen pontoon bridges spanned the water. Infantry and engineers poured ashore, unloading staff cars and light field pieces. Half a mile away the first soldiers were already moving along the railroad line into the town.

Mannock watched a column of infantry march up the road towards them. When they drew nearer he realized that at least half of them were civilians, carrying no weapons or webbing, the women with small red booklets in their hands. On poles over their heads they held giant blown-up photographs of party leaders and generals. A motorcycle and sidecar combination mounting a light machine-gun forced its way past the column, and then stalled in the verge. Chanting together, a group of women and soldiers pushed it free. Together they stamped on after it, bellowing and cheering.

As the motorcycle approached, Mannock waited for the machine-gun to open fire at them. Forbis was crouched behind a fuel drum, frowning over his sights. His large eyes looked like over-boiled eggs. A tic fluttered the right corner of his mouth, as if he were babbling some sub-vocal rosary to himself. Then in a sudden moment of lucidity he turned the shotgun at the motorcycle, but with a roar the machine swerved around Mannock and accelerated towards the town.

Mannock turned to watch it, but a man running past collided with him. Mannock caught his slim shoulders in his hands and set the man on his feet. He looked down into a familiar sallow face, overlit eyes he had last seen staring at him through the bars of a cell.

'Hathaway, you crazy ...'

Before Mannock could hold him he broke away and ran towards the approaching column striding up the dirt road. He stopped a few feet from the leading pair of infantrymen and shouted some greeting to them. One of the men, an officer Mannock guessed, though none of the soldiers wore insignia, glanced at him, then reached out and pushed him to one side. Within a moment he was swallowed by the melée of gong-beating and chanting soldiers. Buffeted from one shoulder to the next, he lost his balance and fell, stood up and began to wave again at the faces passing him, trying to catch their attention.

Then Mannock too was caught up in the throng. The drab quilted uniforms, stained by the dust and sweat of half a continent, pushed past him, forcing him on to the verge. The shotgun was knocked out of his hands, kicked about in the breaking earth by a score of feet, then picked up and tossed on to the back of a cart. A troupe of young women surrounded Mannock, staring up at him without any curiosity as they chanted their slogans. Most of them were little more than children, with earnest mannequin-like faces under close-cropped hair.

Realizing what had happened, Mannock pulled Forbis from the ditch. No one had tried to take his shotgun from Forbis, and the salesman clung to it like a child. Mannock twisted the weapon out of his hands.

'Can't you understand?' he shouted. 'They're not interested in us! They're not interested at all!'

The Comsat Angels

When I first heard about the assignment, in the summer of 1968, I did my best to turn it down. Charles Whitehead, producer of B.B.C.-TVs science programme, *Horizon*, asked me to fly over to France with him and record a press conference being held by a fourteen-year-old child prodigy, Georges Duval, who was attracting attention in the Paris newspapers. The film would form part of *Horizon*'s new series, which I was scripting, 'The Expanding Mind', about the role of communications satellites and data-processing devices in the so-called information explosion. What annoyed me was this insertion of irrelevant and sensational material into an otherwise serious programme.

'Charles, you'll destroy the whole thing,' I protested across his desk that morning. 'These child prodigies are all the same. Either they simply have some freak talent or they're being manipulated by ambitious parents. Do you honestly believe this boy is a genius?'

'He *might* be, James. Who can say?' Charles waved a plump hand at the contact prints of orbiting satellites pinned to the walls. 'We're doing a programme about advanced communications systems – if they have any justification at all, it's that they bring rare talents like this one to light.'

'Rubbish – these prodigies have been exposed time and again. They bear the same relation to true genius that a cross-channel swimmer does to a lunar astronaut.'

In the end, despite my protests, Charles won me over, but I was still sceptical when we flew to Orly Airport the next morning. Every two or three years there were reports of some newly discovered child genius. The pattern was always the same: the prodigy had mastered chess at the age of three, Sanskrit and calculus at six, Einstein's General Theory of Relativity at twelve. The universities and conservatoires of America and Europe opened their doors.

For some reason, though, nothing ever came of these precocious talents. Once the parents, or an unscrupulous commercial sponsor, had squeezed the last drop of publicity out of the child, his so-called genius seemed to evaporate and he vanished into oblivion.

'Do you remember Minou Drouet?' I asked Charles as we drove from Orly. 'A child prodigy of a few years back. Cocteau read her poems and said, "Every child is a genius *except* Minou Drouet." '

'James, relax ... Like all scientists, you can't bear anything that challenges your own prejudices. Let's wait until we see him. He might surprise us.'

He certainly did, though not as we expected.

Georges Duval lived with his widowed mother in the small town of Montereau, on the Seine thirty miles south of Paris. As we drove across the cobbled square past the faded police prefecture, it seemed an unlikely birthplace for another Darwin, Freud or Curie. However, the Duvals' house was an expensively built white-walled villa overlooking a placid arm of the river. A well-tended lawn ran down to a vista of swans and water-meadows.

Parked in the drive was the location truck of the film unit we had hired, and next to it a radio van from Radio-Television-Française and a Mercedes with a *Paris-Match* sticker across the rear window. Sound cables ran across the gravel into a kitchen window. A sharp-faced maid led us without ado towards the press conference. In the lounge, four rows of gilt chairs brought in from the Hôtel de Ville faced a mahogany table by the windows. Here a dozen cameramen were photographing Madame Duval, a handsome woman of thirty-five with calm grey eyes, arms circumspectly folded below two strands of pearls. A trio of solemn-faced men in formal suits protected her from the technicians setting up microphones and trailing their cables under the table.

Already, fifteen minutes before Georges Duval appeared, I felt there was something bogus about the atmosphere. The three dark-suited men – the Director of Studies at the Sorbonne, a senior bureaucrat from the French Ministry of Education, and a representative of the Institut Pascal, a centre of advanced study – gave the conference an overstuffed air only slightly eased by the presence of the local mayor, a homely figure in a greasy suit, and the boy's schoolmaster, a lantern-jawed man hunched around his pipe.

Needless to say, when Georges Duval arrived, he was a total disappointment. Accompanied by a young priest, the family counsellor, he took his seat behind the table, bowing to the three officials and giving his mother a dutiful buss on the cheek. As the lights came on and the cameras began to turn, his eyes stared down at us without embarrassment.

Georges Duval was then fourteen, a slim-shouldered boy small for his age, self-composed in a grey flannel suit. His face was pale and anaemic, hair plastered down to hide his huge bony forehead. He kept his hands in his pockets, concealing his over-large wrists. What struck me immediately was the lack of any emotion or expression on his face, as if he had left his mind in the next room, hard at work on some intricate problem.

Professor Leroux of the Sorbonne opened the press conference. Georges had first come to light when he had taken his mathematics degree at thirteen, the youngest since Descartes. Leroux described Georges's career: reading at the age of two, by nine he had passed his full matriculation exam – usually taken at fifteen or sixteen.

As a vacation hobby he had mastered English and German, by eleven had passed the diploma of the Paris Conservatoire in music theory, by twelve was working for his degree. He had shown a precocious interest in molecular biology, and already corresponded with biochemists at Harvard and Cambridge.

While this familiar catalogue was being unfolded, Georges's eyes, below that large carapace of a skull, showed not a glimmer of emotion. Now and then he glanced at a balding young man in a soft grey suit sitting by himself in the front row. At the time I thought he was Georges's elder brother – he had the same high bony temples and closed face. Later, however, I discovered that he had a very different role.

Questions were invited for Georges. These followed the usual pattern – what did he think of Vietnam, the space-race, the psychedelic scene, miniskirts, girls, Brigitte Bardot? In short, not a question of a serious nature. Georges answered in good humour, stating that outside his studies he had no worthwhile opinions. His voice was firm and reasonably modest, but he looked more and more bored by the conference, and as soon as it broke up, he joined the young man in the front row. Together they left the room, the same abstracted look on their faces that one sees in the insane, as if crossing our own universe at a slight angle.

While we made our way out, I talked to the other journalists. Georges's father had been an assembly worker at the Renault plant in Paris; neither he nor Madame Duval was in the least educated, and the house, into which the widow and son had moved only two months earlier, was paid for by a large research foundation. Evidently there were unseen powers standing guard over Georges Duval. He apparently never played with the boys from the town.

As we drove away, Charles Whitehead said slyly: 'I notice you didn't ask any questions yourself.'

'The whole thing was a complete set-up. We

might as well have been interviewing De Gaulle.'

'Perhaps we were.'

'You think the General may be behind all this?'

'It's possible. Let's face it, if the boy *is* outstanding, it makes it more difficult for him to go off and work for Du Pont or I.B.M.'

'But is he? He was intelligent, of course, but all the same, I'll bet you that three years from now no one will even remember him.'

After we returned to London my curiosity came back a little. In the Air France bus to the TV Centre at White City I scanned the children on the pavement. Without a doubt none of them had the maturity and intelligence of Georges Duval. Two mornings later, when I found myself still thinking about Georges, I went up to the research library.

As I turned through the clippings, going back twenty years, I made an interesting discovery. Starting in 1948, I found that a major news story about a child prodigy came up once every two years. The last celebrity had been Bobby Silverberg, a fifteen-year-old from Tampa, Florida. The photographs in the *Look*, *Paris-Match* and *Oggi* profiles might have been taken of Georges Duval. Apart from the American setting, every ingredient was the same: the press conference, TV cameras, presiding officials, the high-school principal, doting mother—and the young genius himself, this time with a crew-cut and nothing to hide that high bony skull. There were two college degrees already passed, post-graduate fellowships offered by M.I.T., Princeton and CalTech.

And then what?

'That was nearly three years ago,' I said to Judy Walsh, my secretary. 'What's he doing now?'

She flicked through the index cards, then shook her head. 'Nothing. I suppose he's taking another degree at a university somewhere.'

'He's already got two degrees. By now he should have come up with a faster-than-light drive or a method of synthesizing life.'

'He's only seventeen. Wait until he's a little older.'

'Older? You've given me an idea. Let's go back to the beginning – 1948.'

Judy handed me the bundle of clippings. *Life* magazine had picked up the story of Gunther Bergman, the first post-war prodigy, a seventeen-year-old Swedish youth whose pale, over-large eyes stared out from the photographs. An unusual feature was the presence at the graduation ceremony at Uppsala University of three representatives from the Nobel Foundation. Perhaps because he was older than Silverberg and Georges Duval, his intellectual achievements seemed prodigious. The degree he was collecting was his third; already he had done original research in radio-astronomy, helping to identify the unusual radio-sources that a decade later were termed 'quasars'.

'A spectacular career in astronomy seems guaranteed. It should be easy to track him down. He'll be what? thirty-seven now, professor at least, well on his way to a Nobel Prize.'

We searched through the professional directories, telephoned Greenwich Observatory and the London Secretariat of the World Astronomical Federation.

No one had heard of Gunther Bergman.

'Right, where is he?' I asked Judy when we had exhausted all lines of inquiry. 'For heaven's sake, it's twenty years; he should be world-famous by now.'

'Perhaps he's dead.'

'That's possible.' I gazed down pensively at Judy's quizzical face. 'Put in a call to the Nobel Foundation. In fact, clear your desk and get all the international directories we can up here. We're going to make the Comsats sing.'

Three weeks later, when I carried my bulky briefcase into Charles Whitehead's office, there was an electric spring in my step.

Charles eyed me warily over his glasses. 'James, I hear you've been hard on the trail of our missing geniuses. What have you got?'

'A new programme.'

'New? We've already got Georges Duval listed in *Radio Times*.'

'For how long?' I pulled a chair up to his desk and opened my briefcase, then spread the dozen files in front of him. 'Let me put you in the picture. Judy and I have been back to 1948. In those twenty years there have been eleven cases of so-called geniuses. Georges Duval is the twelfth.'

I placed the list in front of him.

1948 Gunther Bergman (Uppsala, Sweden)
1950 Jaako Litmanen (Vaasa, Finland)
1952 John Warrender (Kansas City, U.S.A.)
1953 Arturo Bandini (Bologna, Italy)
1955 Gesai Ray (Calcutta, India)
1957 Giuliano Caldare (Palermo, Sicily)
1958 Wolfgang Herter (Cologne, Germany)
1960 Martin Sherrington (Canterbury, England)
1962 Josef Oblensky (Leningrad, U.S.S.R.)
1964 Yen Hsi Shan (Wuhan, China)
1965 Robert Silverberg (Tampa, U.S.A.)
1968 Georges Duval (Montereau, France)

Charles studied the list, now and then patting his forehead with a floral handkerchief. 'Frankly, apart from Georges Duval, the names mean absolutely nothing.'

'Isn't that strange? There's enough talent there to win all the Nobel Prizes three times over.'

'Have you tried to trace them?'

I let out a cry of pain. Even the placid Judy gave a despairing shudder. 'Have we tried? My God, we've done nothing else. Charles, apart from checking a hundred directories and registers, we've contacted the original magazines and news agencies, checked with the universities that originally offered them scholarships, talked on the overseas lines to the B.B.C. reporters in New York, Delhi and Moscow.'

'And? What do they know about them?'

'Nothing. A complete blank.'

Charles shook his head doggedly. 'They must be somewhere. What about the universities they were supposed to go to?'

'Nothing there, either. It's a curious thing, but not one of them actually went on to a university. We've contacted the senates of nearly fifty universities. Not a mention of them. They took external degrees while still at school, but after that they severed all connections with the academic world.'

Charles sat forward over the list, holding it like a portion of some treasure map. 'James, it looks as if you're going to win your bet. Somehow they all petered out in late adolescence. A sudden flaring of intelligence backed by prodigious memory, not matched by any real creative spark ... that's it, I suppose – none of them was a genius.'

'As a matter of fact, I think they all were.' Before he could stop me I went on. 'Forget that for the moment. Whether or not they had genius is irrelevant. Certainly they had intellects vastly beyond the average, IQs of two hundred, enormous scholastic talents in a wide range of subjects. They had a sudden burst of fame and exposure and –'

'They vanished into thin air. What are you suggesting – some kind of conspiracy?'

'In a sense, yes.'

Charles handed me the list. 'Come off it. Do you really mean that a sinister government bureau has smuggled them off, they're slaving away now on some superweapon?'

'It's possible, but I doubt it.' I took a packet of photographs from the second folder. 'Have a look at them.'

Charles picked up the first. 'Ah, there's Georges. He looks older here, those TV cameras are certainly ageing.'

'It's not Georges Duval. It's Oblensky, the Russian boy, taken six years ago. Quite a resemblance, though.' I spread the twelve photographs on the table top. Charles moved along the half-circle, comparing the over-large eyes and bony foreheads, the same steady gaze.

'Wait a minute! Are you sure this isn't Duval?' Charles picked up Oblensky's photograph and pointed to the figure of a young man in a light grey suit standing behind some mayoral official in a Leningrad parlour. '*He* was at Duval's press conference, sitting right in front of us.'

I nodded to Judy. 'You're right, Charles. And he's not only in that photo.' I pulled together the photographs of Bobby Silverberg, Herter and Martin Sherrington. In each one the same balding figure in the dove-grey suit was somewhere in the background, his over-sharp eyes avoiding the camera lens. 'No university admits to knowing him, nor do Shell, Philips, General Motors or a dozen other big international companies. Of course, there are other organizations he might be a talent scout for ... '

Charles had stood up, and was slowly walking around his desk. 'Such as the C.I.A.—you think he may be recruiting talent for some top-secret Government think-tank? It's unlikely, but—'

'What about the Russians?' I cut in. 'Or the Chinese? Let's face it, eleven young men have vanished into thin air. What happened to them?'

Charles stared down at the photographs. 'The strange thing is that I vaguely recognize all these faces. Those bony skulls, and those eyes ... somewhere. Look, James, we may have the makings of a new programme here. This English prodigy, Martin Sherrington, he should be easy to track down. Then the German, Herter. Find them and we may be on to something.'

We set off for Canterbury the next morning. The address, which I had been given by a friend who was science editor of the *Daily Express*, was on a housing estate behind the big General Electric radio and television plant on the edge of the city. We drove past the lines of grey-brick houses until we found the Sherringtons' at the end of a row. Rising out of the remains of a greenhouse was a huge ham operator's radio mast, its stay-wires snapped and rusting. In the eight years since his tremendous mind had revealed itself to the local grammar-school master, Martin Sherrington might have gone off to the ends of the world, to Cape Kennedy, the Urals or Peking.

In fact, not only were neither Martin nor his parents there, but it took us all of two days to find anyone who even remembered them at all. The present tenants of the house, a frayed-looking couple, had been there two years; and before them a large family of criminal inclinations who had been forced out by bailiffs and police. The headmaster of the grammar-school had retired to Scotland. Fortunately the school matron remembered Martin – 'a brilliantly clever boy, we were all very proud of him. To tell the truth, though, I can't say we felt much affection for him; he didn't invite it.' She knew nothing of Mrs Sherrington, and as for the boy's father, they assumed he had died in the war.

Finally, thanks to a cashier at the accounts office of the local electric company, we found where Mrs Sherrington had moved.

As soon as I saw that pleasant white-walled villa in its prosperous suburb on the other side of Canterbury, I felt that the trail was warming. Something about the crisp gravel and large, well-trimmed garden reminded me of another house – Georges Duval's near Paris.

From the roof of my car parked next to the hedge we

watched a handsome, strong-shouldered woman strolling in the rose garden.

'She's come up in the world,' I commented. 'Who pays for this pad?'

The meeting was curious. This rather homely, quietly dressed woman in her late thirties gazed at us across the silver tea-set like a tamed Mona Lisa. She told us that we had absolutely no chance of interviewing Martin on television.

'So much interest in your son was roused at the time, Mrs Sherrington. Can you tell us about his subsequent academic career? Which university did he go to?'

'His education was completed privately.' As for his present whereabouts, she believed he was now abroad, working for a large international organization whose name she was not at liberty to divulge.

'Not a government department, Mrs Sherrington?'

She hesitated, but only briefly. 'I am told the organization is intimately connected with various governments, but I have no real knowledge.'

Her voice was over-precise, as if she were hiding her real accent. As we left, I realized how lonely her life was; but as Judy remarked, she had probably been lonely ever since Martin Sherrington had first learned to speak.

Our trip to Germany was equally futile. All traces of Wolfgang Herter had vanished from the map. A few people in the small village near the Frankfurt autobahn remembered him, and the village postman said that Frau Herter had moved to Switzerland, to a lakeside villa near Lucerne. A woman of modest means and education, but the son had no doubt done very well.

I asked one or two questions.

Wolfgang's father? Frau Herter had arrived with the child just after the war; the husband had probably perished in one of the nameless prison-camps or battlegrounds of World War II.

The balding man in the light grey suit? Yes, he had definitely come to the village, helping Frau Herter arrange her departure.

'Back to London,' I said to Judy. 'This needs bigger resources than you and I have.'

As we flew back Judy said: 'One thing I don't understand. Why have the fathers always disappeared?'

'A good question. Putting it crudely, love, a unique genetic coupling produced these twelve boys. It almost looks as if someone has torn the treasure map in two and kept one half. Think of the stock bank they're building up, enough sperm on ice in a eugenic cocktail to repopulate the entire planet.'

This nightmare prospect was on my mind when I walked into Charles Whitehead's office the next morning. It was the first time I had seen Charles in his shirtsleeves. To my surprise, he brushed aside my apologies, then beckoned me to the huge spread of photographs pinned to the plaster wall behind his desk. The office was a clutter of newspaper cuttings and blown-up newsreel stills. Charles was holding a magnifying glass over a photograph of President Johnson and McNamara at a White House reception.

'While you were gone we've been carrying out our own search,' he said. 'If it's any consolation, we couldn't trace any of them at first.'

'Then you have found them? Where?'

'Here.' He gestured at the dozens of photographs. 'Right in front of our noses. We're looking at them every day.'

He pointed to a news agency photograph of a Kremlin reception for Premier Ulbricht of East Germany. Kosygin and Brezhnev were there, Soviet President Podgorny talking to the Finnish Ambassador, and a crowd of twenty party functionaries.

'Recognize anyone? Apart from Kosygin and company?'

'The usual bunch of hatchet-faced waiters these people like to surround themselves with. Wait a minute, though.'

Charles's finger had paused over a quiet-faced young man with a high dolichocephalic head, standing at Kosygin's elbow. Curiously, the Soviet Premier's face was turned towards him rather than to Brezhnev.

'Oblensky – the Russian prodigy. What's he doing with Kosygin? He looks like an interpreter.'

'Between Kosygin and Brezhnev? Hardly. I've checked with the B.B.C. and Reuter correspondents in Moscow. They've seen him around quite a bit. He never says anything in public, but the important men always talk to *him*.'

I put down the photograph. 'Charles, get on to the Foreign Office and the U.S. Embassy. It makes sense – all eleven of them are probably there, in the Soviet Union.'

'Relax. That's what we thought. But have a look at these.'

The next picture had been taken at a White House meeting between Johnson, McNamara and General Westmoreland discussing U.S. policy in Vietnam. There were the usual aides, secretaries and Secret Service men out on the lawn. One face had been ringed, that of a man in his early thirties standing unobtrusively behind Johnson and Westmoreland.

'Warrender – the 1952 genius! *He*'s working for the U.S. Government.'

'More surprises.' Charles guided me around the rest of the photographs. 'You might be interested in these.'

The next showed Pope Paul on the balcony of St Peter's, making his annual 'Urbis et Orbis' – the city and the world – benediction to the huge crowd in the square. Standing beside him were Cardinal Mancini, chief of the Papal Secretariat, and members of his household staff. Obliquely behind the Pope was a man of about thirty wearing what I guessed to be a Jesuit's soutane, large eyes watching Paul with a steady gaze.

L.F.A. – 12

'Bandini, Arturo Bandini,' I commented, recognizing the face. '*Oggi* did a series of features on him. He's moved high in the papal hierarchy.'

'There are few closer to Il Papa, or better loved.'

After that came a photograph of U Thant, taken at a U.N. Security Council meeting during the Cuban missile crisis. Sitting behind the Secretary General was a pale-skinned young Brahmin with a fine mouth and eyes – Gesai Ray, the high-caste Indian who was the only well-born prodigy I had come across.

'Ray is now even higher up on U Thant's staff,' Charles added. 'There's one interesting photograph of him and Warrender together during the Cuban crisis. Warrender was then on J.F.K.'s staff.' He went on casually: 'The year after Oblensky reached the Kremlin, Khrushchev was sacked.'

'So they're in contact? I'm beginning to realize what the Moscow–Washington hot line is really for.'

Charles handed me another still. 'Here's an old friend of yours – our own Martin Sherrington. He's on Professor Lovell's staff at the Jodrell Bank Radio-Observatory. One of the very few not to go into government or big business.'

'Big science, though.' I stared at the quiet, intense face of the elusive Sherrington, aware that someone at Jodrell Bank had deliberately put me off.

'Like Gunther Bergman – he moved to the United States fifteen years ago from Sweden, is now very high up in the NASA command chain. Yen Hsi Shan is the youngest, barely seventeen, but have a look at this.'

The photograph showed Mao Tse-tung and Chou En-lai on the reviewing platform in Peking during the cultural revolution, an immense concourse of teenagers passing below, all holding copies of Mao's *Thoughts* and chanting out slogans. Standing between Mao and Chou was a boy with a fist in the air who was the chief Red Guard.

'Yen Hsi Shan. He's started early,' Charles said. 'One

or two of the others we haven't been able to trace as yet, though we hear Herter is with the giant Zurich-Hamburg banking trust. Jaako Litmanen, the Finnish prodigy, is rumoured to be working for the Soviet space programme.'

'Well, one has to admit it,' I commented, 'they've certainly all made good.'

'Not all.' Charles showed me the last picture, of the Sicilian genius Giuliano Caldare. 'One of them made bad. Caldare emigrated to the United States in 1960, is now in the inner circle of the Cosa Nostra, a coming talent from all one hears.'

I sat down at Charles's desk. 'Right, but what does this prove? It may look like a conspiracy, but given their talents one would expect them to rise in the world.'

'That's putting it mildly. Good God, this bunch only has to take one step forward and they'll be running the entire show.'

'A valid point.' I opened Charles's note-pad. 'We'll revise the programme – agreed? We start off with the Georges Duval conference, follow up with our own discoveries of where the others are, splice in old newsreel material, interviews with the mothers – it'll make quite a programme.'

Or so we hoped.

Needless to say, the programme was never started. Two days later, when I was still organizing the newsreel material, word came down from the head of features that the project was to be shelved. We tried to argue, but the decision was absolute.

Shortly after, my contract with *Horizon* was ended, and I was given the job of doing a new children's series about great inventors. Charles was shunted to 'International Golf'. Of course, it was obvious to both of us that we had come too close for someone's comfort, but there was little we could do about it. Three months later, I made a trip to Jodrell Bank radio-observatory with a party of scientific journalists and had a glimpse of Martin Sherrington, a tall, finely featured man watching with his hard gaze as Professor Lovell held his press conference.

During the next months I carefully followed the newspapers and TV newscasts. If there was a conspiracy of some kind, what were they planning? Here they were, sitting behind the world's great men, hands ready to take the levers of power. But a global dictatorship sounded unlikely. Two of them at least seemed opposed to established authority. Apart from Caldare in the Cosa Nostra, Georges Duval put his musical talents to spectacular use, becoming within less than a year the greatest of the French 'Ye-Ye' singers, eclipsing the Beatles as a leader of the psychedelic youth generation. In the forefront of the world protest movement, he was hated by the police of a dozen countries but idolized by teenagers from Bangkok to Mexico City.

Any collaboration between Georges and Bandini at the Vatican seemed improbable. Besides, nothing that happened in the world at large suggested that members of the group were acting in anything but a benign role: the nuclear confrontation averted during the Cuban missile crisis, the fall of Khrushchev and the Russo-American détente, peace moves in Vietnam, the Vatican's liberalized policy towards birth-control and divorce. Even the Red Guard movement and the chaos it brought could be seen as a subtle means of deflecting Chinese militancy at a time when she might have intervened in Vietnam.

Then, three months later, Charles Whitehead telephoned me.

'There's a report in *Der Spiegel*,' he told me with studied casualness. 'I thought you might be interested. Another young genius has been discovered.'

'Great,' I said. 'We'll do a programme about it. The usual story, I take it?'

'Absolutely. That same forehead and eyes, the mother

who lost her husband years ago, our friend in the villa business. This boy looks really bright, though. An IQ estimated at 300. What a mind.'

'I read the script. The only trouble is, I never got to see the programme. Where is this, by the way?'

'Hebron.'

'Where's that?'

'Near Jerusalem. In Israel.'

'Israel?'

I put the phone down. Somewhere in my mind a tumbler had clicked. Israel! Of course, at last everything made sense. The twelve young men, now occupying positions of power, controlling everything from the U.S., Russian and Chinese governments to satellite policy, international finance, the UN, big science, the youth and protest movement. There was even a Judas, Giuliano Caldare of the Cosa Nostra. It was obvious now. I had always assumed that the twelve were working for some mysterious organization, but in fact they *were* the organization. They were waiting for the moment of arrival. When the child came, he would be prepared for in the right way, watched over by the Comsat relays, hot lines open, the armies of the world immobilized. This time there would be no mistakes.

After an hour I rang Charles back.

'Charles,' I began, 'I know what's happening. Israel ... '

'What are you talking about?'

'Israel. Don't you see, Hebron is near Bethlehem.'

There was an exasperated silence. 'James, for heaven's sake ... You're not suggesting that–'

'Of course. The twelve young men, what else could they be preparing for? And why did the Arab-Israeli war end in only two days? How old is this boy?'

'Thirteen.'

'Let's say another ten years. Good, I had a feeling he would come.'

When Charles protested I handed the receiver to Judy.

As a matter of fact, I am quite certain that I am right. I have seen the photographs of Joshua Herzl taken at his press conference, a slightly difficult lad who rubbed quite a few of the reporters the wrong way. He vanished off the scene shortly afterwards, though no doubt his mother now has a pleasant white-walled villa outside Haifa or Tel Aviv.

And Jodrell Bank is building an enormous new radio-telescope. One day soon we shall be seeing signs in the skies.

The Beach Murders

INTRODUCTION

Readers hoping to solve the mystery of the Beach Murders—involving a Romanoff Princess, a C.I.A. agent, two of his Russian counterparts, and an American limbo dancer—may care to approach it in the form of the card game with which Quimby, the absconding State Department cipher chief, amused himself in his hideaway on the Costa Blanca. The principal clues have therefore been alphabetized. The correct key might well be a familiar phrase, e.g. PLAYMATE OF THE MONTH, *or meaningless, e.g.* qwertyuiop ... *etc. Obviously any number of solutions is possible, and a final answer to the mystery, like the motives and character of Quimby himself, lies forever hidden*

Auto-erotic

As always after her bath, the reflection of her naked body filled the Princess with a profound sense of repose. In the triptych of mirrors above the dressing table she gazed at the endless replicas of herself, the scent of the Guerlain heliotrope soothing her slight migraine. She lowered her arms as the bedroom door opened. Through the faint mist of talcum she recognized the handsome, calculating face of the Russian agent whose photograph she had seen in Statler's briefcase that afternoon.

Brassière

Statler waded through the breaking surf. The left cup of the brassière in his hand was stained with blood. He bent down and washed it in the warm water. The pulsing headlamps of the Mercedes parked below the corniche road lit up the cove. Where the hell was Lydia? Somewhere along the beach a woman with a bloody breast would frighten the wits out of the Russian landing party.

Cordobés
The self-contained face of the bullfighter, part gamin, part Beatle, lay below Quimby as he set out the cards on the balcony table. Whatever else they said about the boy, he never moved his feet. By contrast Raissa was pacing around the bedroom like a tigress in rut. Quimby could hear her wide Slavic hips brushing against his Paisley dressing-gown behind the escritoire. What these obsessives in Moscow and Washington failed to realize was that for once he might have no motive at all.

Drinamyl
Those bloody little capsules, Raissa thought. No wonder the West was dying. Every time she was ready to lure Quimby over to Sir Giles's villa he took one of the tranquillizers, then went down to the sea and talked to the beachniks. At Benidorm he even had the nerve to bring one of the Swedish girls back to the apartment. Hair down to her knees, breasts like thimbles, the immense buttocks of a horse. Ugh.

Embonpoint
The Princess slid the remains of the eclair into her mouth. As she swallowed the pastry she pouted her cream-filled lips at Statler. He lowered his rolled-up copy of *Time Atlantic*, with its photo of Quimby before the House Committee. The dancers moved around the tea-terrace to the soft rhythm of the fox-trot. There was something sensuous, almost sexual, about Manon's compulsive eating of eclairs. This magnificent Serbo-Croat cow, had she any idea what was going to happen to her?

Fata Morgana
Lydia felt his hand move along the plastic zipper of her

dress. She lay on the candlewick bedspread, gazing at the sea and the white sand. Apart from the dotty English milord who had rented the villa to them the place was empty. As Kovarski hesitated the silence seemed to amplify all the uncertainties she had noticed since their arrival at San Juan. The meeting at the nudist colony on the Isle du Levant had not been entirely fortuitous. She reached up and loosened the zip. As her breasts came out she turned to face him. Kovarski was sitting up on one elbow, staring through his Zeiss binoculars at the apartment block three hundred yards along the beach.

Guardia Civil
Quimby watched the olive-uniformed policemen ambling along the shore, their quaint Napoleonic hats shielding their eyes as they scanned the girls on the beach. When it came to the crunch, on whose side would they see themselves – Stat's, the Russians', or his own? Quimby shuffled the Cordobés-backed cards. The platinum-haired call-girl who lived in the next apartment was setting off for Alicante in her pink Fiat. Quimby sipped his whisky. Five minutes earlier he had discovered the concealed aerial of Raissa's transmitter.

Heterodyne
Kovarski was worried. The sight of Raissa's body on the pony skin reminded him that Statler was still to be reckoned with. The piercing whistle from the portable radio confirmed that Raissa had been lying there since dusk. He knelt down, eyes lingering for a last moment on the silver clasps of her Gossard suspenders. He put his finger in her mouth and ran it around her gums, searching for the capsule. A cherry popped into his palm. With a grimace he dropped it into the vodkatini by the radio. He opened Raissa's right hand and from the frozen clasp of her thumb and forefinger removed the capsule. As he read the message his brow furrowed. What the devil had the

Princess to do with Quimby? Was this some insane C.I.A. plot to restore the Romanoffs?

Iguana

The jade reptile shattered on the tiled floor at Sir Giles's feet. With an effort he regained his balance. Pretending to straighten his Old Etonian tie, he touched the painful bruise under his breast-bone. He looked up at the tough, square-jawed face of the American girl. Would she hit him again? She glared at him contemptuously, bare feet planted wide on the pony skin. Ah well, he thought, there had been worse moments. At Dunkirk the bombs falling from the Stukas had made the beach drum like a dancing floor.

Jasmine

Statler gazed at the white salver-shaped flowers in the lobby. Their nacreous petals, bled of all colour, reminded him of Manon's skin, and then of Quimby's large pallid face, with its too-intelligent eyes watching over the sunken cheeks like a snide Buddha's. Was the exchange a fair one, the Princess for the complex, moody cipher chief? He walked out through the revolving doors of the hotel into the bright Alicante sunlight, realizing with a pang that he would never see Manon again.

Kleenex

Raissa bent forwards over the bed. With the ring finger of her right hand she lifted her eyelid. For a moment the elegant mask of her face was contorted like an obscene paroquet's. She tapped the lower lid and the micro-lens jumped on to the tissue. The minute R on its rim shone in the beam of the Anglepoise. She wiped the lenses and placed them in the polarimeter. As the door of the safe opened, revealing the dials of the transmitter, she listened to Quimby singing *Arrivederci Roma* in the bathroom. All that drinamyl and whisky would keep the pig drowsy for at least an hour.

Limbo

The bar had been a mere twelve inches from the floor, Kovarski recollected, as he felt the hard curve of Lydia's iliac crest under the midnight blue stretch pants. For once the nightclub in Benidorm was hushed, everyone watching as this demented American girl with the incredible thighs had edged under the bar, hips jerking to the throb of the juke-box. Kovarski picked his nose, involuntarily thinking about Stat. The C.I.A. man had a face like ice.

Mercedes

The brake servos had gone. Holding the hand-brake, Lydia groped behind Kovarski's chest for the off-side door handle. The Russian lay against the sill, his handsome face beginning to sag like the first slide of an avalanche. As the door opened he fell backwards on to the gravel. Lydia released the hand-brake and let the car roll forwards. When Kovarski had gone she wound up the window, elegantly starred by the bullet which had passed through the door. She flashed the headlamps for the last time and pressed the starter.

Neapolitan

Raissa finished off the remains of Quimby's ice-cream with the eager lips of a child. In three hours they would be six fathoms under the Mediterranean, due to surface for the first time in the Baltic. She would miss the sunlight, and the small, dark Spaniards with their melancholy eyes following her down the dusty street to the bodega. In the end it would be worth it. Throw away the Man-Tan, as Kovarski often quoted to her in his mock-Yevtushenko, the sky will soon be full of suns.

Oceanid

For a moment Manon realized that Kovarski was undecided whether to rape or kill her. She backed into the bathroom, her left hand covering her powdered breasts. The trapped steam billowed into Kovarski's face. He goggled at her like an insane student in a Dostoevski novel. He stepped across the cork bathmat and took her elbow in a surprisingly tender gesture. Then the alabaster soap-dish caught her on the side of the head. A second later she was lying in a hot mess in the bath, Kovarski's arms moving over her head like pistons.

Poseidon

Quimby handled the bottle of Black Label with a respect due their long acquaintance. The proto-Atlantic ocean had covered all North America and Europe except for Scotland, leaving intact a percolation system 300 million years old. As he filled his glass he watched Sir Giles's villa on the bluff above the cove. The swarthy Russian and his American beatnik had moved in yesterday. No doubt Stat was at the Carlton in Alicante. Quimby set out the cards for the last game. The hand would be hard to play, but luckily he was still dealing.

Quietus

Statler was dying in the dark surf. As the Russian bosun let him drift away in the shallow water he was thinking of the Princess and her immense brown nipples. Had she borne a child then, keeping alive the fading memories of the Austro-Hungarian Empire? The burning wreck of the Mercedes shone through the water, illuminating the bodies of the two Russians being dragged towards the dinghy. Statler lay back in the cold water as his blood ran out into the sea.

Remington

Lydia knelt by Kovarski's Travel-Riter. In the courtyard below the bedroom window Sir Giles was setting off for Alicante in his battered Citroën. That twitching old goat, did the English ever think about anything else? She removed the hood from the typewriter, then peered at the new ribbon she had inserted while Kovarski was in San Juan. The imprint of the letters shone in the sunlight. She jotted them on to the bridge pad, then tore off the sheet and slipped it into the left cup of her brassière.

Smith & Wesson
Kovarski blundered through the darkness among the dunes. Below him the surf broke like a lace shawl on the beach. The whole operation was going to pieces. By now Raissa should have been here with Quimby. He climbed the slope up to the Mercedes. As he felt for the pistol in the glove compartment something moved on the gravel behind him. The gun-flash lit up the interior of the car. Kovarski fell sideways across the seat. The second bullet passed through his chest and went on into the off-side door.

Tranquillizer
Statler opened the capsule and drew out the folded tissue. In Raissa's untouched vodkatini the rice paper flared like a Japanese water-flower. He fished it out with the toothpick and laid it on the salver. So this was how they made contact. He looked down at the body on the pony skin and smiled to himself. With luck Kovarski would literally eat his own words. As he turned the Russian girl over with his foot the cherry popped from her mouth. He pushed it back between her lips and went over to the Travel-Riter.

U.V. Lamp
With a sigh the Princess dropped the goggles into the douche-bag on the dressing table. In spite of her efforts, the months of summer bathing on the Côte d'Azur before her meeting with Stat, her skin remained as white as the jasmine blossoms in the lobby. In her veins ran the haemophilic blood of the Romanoffs, yet the time to

revenge Ekaterinburg had passed. Did Stat realize this?

Vivaldi
Lydia tuned in Radio Algiers with a wet forefinger. The French had left some damned good records behind. She stood on the pony skin, admiring her tough, man-like hips as she dried herself after the swim. Her sharp nails caressed the cold skin of her breasts. Then she noticed Sir Giles's marmoset-like face peering at her through the fronds of the miniature palm beside the bedroom door.

Wave Speed
6,000 metres per second, enough to blow Stat straight through the rear window of the Merc. Kovarski lifted the hood and lowered the bomb into the slot behind the battery. Over his shoulder he peered into the darkness across the sea. Two miles out, where the deep water began, the submarine would be waiting, the landing party crouched by their dinghy under the conning-tower. He tightened the terminals, licking the blood from the reopened wound on his hand. The Princess had packed a lot of muscle under that incredible ivory skin.

XF–169
The Lockheed performance data would make a useful bonus, Raissa reflected as she slipped her long legs into the stretch pants. The charge account at GUM and the dacha in the Crimea were becoming a distinct possibility. The door opened behind her. Siphon in hand, Quimby stared at her half-naked figure. Without thinking, she put her hands over her breasts. For once his face registered an expression of surprising intelligence.

Yardley
Sir Giles helped himself to Statler's after-shave lotion. He looked down at the Princess. Even allowing for her size, the quantity of expressed blood was unbelievable. His

small face was puckered with embarrassment as he met her blank eyes staring up at the shower fitment. He listened to the distant sounds of traffic coming through the empty suite. He turned on the shower. As the drops spattered on the red skin the magnificence of her white body made his mind reel.

Zeitgeist

The great fans of the *guardia civil* Sikorsky beat the air over the apartment block. Quimby bent down and retrieved two of the cards from the tiled floor. Below, along the beach road, the Spanish speed cops were converging on the wreck of the Mercedes. Quimby sat back as the helicopter battered away through the darkness. All in all, everything had worked out. The face of Cordobés still regarded him from the backs of the cards. A full moon was coming up over the Sierra. In the Alicante supermarket the hips of the counter girls shook to Trini Lopez. In the bodega wine was only ten pesetas a litre, and the man with the deck still controlled the play.

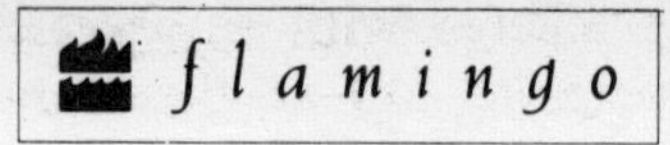
flamingo